DON PENDLETON's EXECUTIONER

MACK BOLAN

Day of Mourning

A GOLD EAGLE BOOK FROM
WORLDWIDE

TORONTO • NEW YORK • LONDON • PARIS
AMSTERDAM • STOCKHOLM • HAMBURG
ATHENS • MILAN • TOKYO • SYDNEY

First edition February 1984

ISBN 0-373-61062-9

Special thanks and acknowledgment to
Stephen Mertz for his contributions to this work.

Printed in Canada

The world dies 'twixt every heartbeat,
and is born again
in each new perception of the mind.
For each of us,
the order of life is to *perceive* and *perish* and
       perceive again,
and who can say which is which—
for every human experience builds a new world
in its own image—
and death itself is but an unusual perception.
Live large that you may experience large
and thus, hopefully, die large.

       —A *soldada*'s final words.
       Translated from the Spanish
       for Bolan in *Miami Massacre*

Dedicated to the governors of New York
and New Jersey who, independent of
Washington, took it upon themselves to bar
Soviet Foreign Minister Andrei Gromyko
from landing in his Aeroflot plane at
Newark or Kennedy international airports
following the shooting down of KAL Flight 007.

1

*In the beginning, it was like any of the other missions
in this government-sanctioned new war against world
terrorism: Mack Bolan, the Executioner, now known
as Colonel John Macklin Phoenix, the stony man of
Stony Man, racing toward another confrontation
with dark forces. . . .*

The AV-8B Advanced Harrier skimmed the endless expanse of the choppy Atlantic at a snappy 600
mph. Jack Grimaldi was behind the controls of the
Vertical Short Takeoff and Landing combat jet,
heading on a southeasterly course three hundred
miles off the northern coast of Brazil. The Marine
Corps' state of the art VSTOL aircraft was equipped
with full cannon and missile capability.

Grimaldi's passenger was a big, icy-eyed man outfitted in scuba gear.

Mack Bolan, in the seat behind Grimaldi, felt
wrapped in the steady low-pitched whine of the jet's
engines.

A gray cloud ceiling melded with the turbulent
ocean on the near horizon beyond the Harrier's
Plexiglas.

Bolan jarred forward against his shoulder harness

as Grimaldi, a longtime ally in the Executioner's old and new wars, slacked off sharply on the mighty aircraft's forward thrust.

Grimaldi then brought the Harrier to a stationary hover at fifty feet above the roiling sea.

The pilot's voice crackled through Bolan's headset.

"Radar beep, forty-seven miles due south. Right on the money, Striker. Do we hit 'em?"

"After you patch me through to Stony Man," growled Bolan. "I want a status report on Phoenix Force."

"Check. Patching you through now," came Grimaldi's voice.

This Harrier boasted a direct communications linkup to a satellite relay capable of establishing near-instant voice contact with the stateside Stony Man control base.

Stony Man Farm was a rolling 160-acre estate in the Blue Ridge Mountains of Virginia, three thousand miles away.

The "farm" was in reality the command center of the Phoenix program, a covert operation unrecorded in official files, headed by Mack Bolan. The facility was the headquarters of the most formidable security force ever assembled, operating with full government support.

At this moment Hal Brognola, Stony Man's liaison with the White House, and April Rose, the farm's overseer and mission controller, would be monitoring the progress of both Bolan and Grimaldi, and the men of Phoenix Force, who were on their way to rendezvous with the Harrier.

Upcoming was the Executioner's first deep-sea action.

Underwater combat had been a part of Bolan's Stony Man training that he had not had to use until now. The warrior in scuba black was ready with the know-how and the best equipment and weaponry for this mission.

Bolan could not afford to wait for Phoenix Force. The numbers were falling too fast. But at least he would know their ETA, and that could make a difference.

Bolan noted the lengthy pause from the cockpit.

"What is it, Jack?"

"I'm not sure," crackled the pilot's voice. "We seem to have a communications breakdown."

"Did you try the alternate frequencies?"

"Both of 'em. All I get is static."

"Is it us?"

"Negative. Other channels are loud and clear. I can pick up any frequency from anywhere with this baby. But no Stony Man."

"That radar beep. Is it stationary?"

"Affirmative. The coordinates are right. We're too damn far out for fishing. Anything else would be moving."

"Anything else on the screen?"

"Nothing within range. That doesn't mean our target won't have backup. It would sure help to have Phoenix Force along."

"You know the numbers, Jack. There's no time. Close in on the target."

"We thunder it?"

"Affirmative," growled Bolan. "Do it now."

Grimaldi punched the Harrier's afterburners. Another jolt and the jet shot forward, again at full throttle. The ocean below became a sleek blur like dark glass.

Bolan was concerned about the communications failure. But he was trying not to let it affect his combat consciousness as he prepared for the impending confrontation in a watery hellground.

Bolan could not remember Stony Man Farm ever having a communications-system malfunction.

The Executioner and his Stony Man combat units, Able Team and Phoenix Force, were supported by an intel and communications linkup masterminded and run by Aaron "The Bear" Kurtzman. He was a perfectionist. Nothing Kurtzman touched at Stony Man had ever gone wrong.

Yet here were Bolan and Grimaldi jetting into hot contact with the enemy, and communications were blacked out.

Bolan was used to working on his own. He preferred it that way. Give him at most one or two allies, and this warrior felt confident in tackling any mission.

Many times during his war against terrorism, and that former life of warring against the Mafia, the Executioner had pulled off his most stunning victories with just his weapons. Bolan sometimes missed those days; more and more often lately, it seemed. He knew that it was not absolutely necessary for him to have a communications link with Stony Man at this time.

Nevertheless the unexpected breakdown did concern him.

What's wrong at Stony Man? he wondered.

The flight from Central America had gone off without a hitch. The mission had been a tough, violent one. Colonel Phoenix and Grimaldi had been heading home when Brognola contacted Bolan in flight.

The big guy's senses had leveled into a postcombat cool. He could feel weariness pestering to be acknowledged. His soul felt tired, and so did his body. That changed when he and Grimaldi had listened to Brognola's descrambled message.

"We may already be too late, Striker." Brognola had sounded harried. "A terrorist coalition has bankrolled purchase of a top-secret nuclear device from an as yet undetermined European source. A hell bomb the size of a goddamn suitcase was shipped on a Liberian freighter, but the ship went down in a storm. Precautions were taken, and there's a fifty-fifty chance the nuclear device is still intact in a waterproof container."

"Do we have coordinates on the site?"

"We do. The ship's radioman was in touch with the terrorists before radio contact was broken and the ship went down. We were fed the information by a mole in one of the terrorist groups."

"What's the official status on the sinking?"

"Maritime SOP hasn't turned up a thing," said Hal. "The terrorist group already has a salvage operation under way. A Soviet-trained frogman crew set out from Belém on the Brazilian coast yesterday afternoon. We learned of all this only a few minutes ago. The terrorists have their whole network trip-wired for this thing, and the intel came to us second-hand. That's why it took so long for the news to travel. The CIA has lost contact with two of their people inside the coalition. They've already written them off as having been terminated.''

Brognola had then given the coordinates to Bolan and Grimaldi.

The Stony warrior and his pilot had briefly touched down at a secret U.S. military air base in Honduras for refueling, equipment and ordnance. Then this fast flight southeast.

It was Brognola's idea to have Phoenix Force flown in to back up the Executioner and Grimaldi.

Grimaldi's voice crackled again.

"Here we go, Striker. Get ready."

Bolan saw the target at that instant: a 100-foot commercial deep-sea fishing vessel, bobbing on the gray Atlantic.

The Harrier lanced in with its specially mounted machine guns yammering away.

The deck crew never knew what hit them as the Harrier flashed by overhead like a giant firebreathing bird skimming the water surface for food. The pounding machine guns strafed every inch of the deck, filling the air with splintering wood and shreds of tumbling bodies and blood as blistering lead killed every living thing.

Then the Harrier banked in a smooth curve. Grimaldi eased the warplane back to a stationary hover off the port bow of the boat.

Nothing moved down there. Lifeless bodies were sprawled all over the pulverized deck. The boat rode the rolling crests of the waves like a ghost ship.

"Here we are, Striker," crackled Grimaldi.

"Hold it right here, Jack."

The Harrier maintained stationary hold.

The hellbringer in the passenger seat slid back the Plexiglas cowling, then stood to begin a final equipment check.

Brognola's intel was that the Liberian freighter had touched bottom in five hundred feet of water.

Conventional scuba-diving gear would not be practical below three hundred feet, so the Executioner was snugly togged in a Deep Diving System suit, courtesy of a Marine Corps scuba unit in Honduras.

The space-age scuba suit worn by Bolan was made of a special neoprene with an alloy helmet featuring a closed-circuit rebreather unit that eliminated telltale air bubbles from the helmet and adjusted the pressure not only within the suit, but within the sinuses and other internal air spaces within the diver's body. The suit's safety depth: twelve hundred feet.

But this scuba suit did have its shortcomings. It was designed for staying down no more than forty minutes, and Bolan would need to spend time in a decompression chamber when he came up.

Bolan activated the DDS and adjusted the harness on his air tanks.

He was armed with a sheathed knife at his left hip and a specially designed shark gun. At one end of the underwater weapon was a rod capable of sending off a six-thousand-volt electrical charge. The gun also fired 41.8mm bullets propelled by carbon dioxide through a barrel above the shock rod. The bullets were designed to explode on contact.

Bolan climbed onto a wing of the Harrier and moved cautiously away from the fuselage, avoiding the jet engines to either side of the cockpit.

"Last chance to change your mind," warned Grimaldi.

"You know better, Jack," replied the blitzer on the wing. "Keep trying to raise Stony Man. Black out communications with me once I'm under. Try to intercept any signals from down below. That's the enemy. We still don't know if they have backup standing by."

"And you come up in forty minutes."

"Precisely forty minutes."

"And if you don't make it up in forty?"

"Then I won't be making it," Bolan replied in a matter-of-fact tone.

"We've had no goddamn recon of what's waiting for you down there," Grimaldi said suddenly. "I don't like it, Striker."

"Neither do I. What's that have to do with anything?" was Bolan's parting shot.

He adjusted his fins. He was ready.

Bolan again felt a twitch of concern at the communications breakdown with Stony Man Farm. And where the hell was Phoenix Force?

He knew a nuclear bomb in the hands of terrorists was unthinkable in the already bloody arena of Central and South American political terror that was advancing year by year toward America's border.

He put those thoughts aside. It was time for action.

"Good luck, soldier," said Grimaldi.

The Executioner gave a clenched fist and thumbs-up sign to the pilot, then stepped off the Harrier's wing.

Bolan plummeted a fast twenty feet into the frigid, turbulent depths of the sea, disappearing from Grimaldi's sight.

2

Bolan sliced smoothly into the dark underwater void. The raging turbulence of the ocean's surface and the whine of the Harrier faded to throbbing rumbles, then to nothing.

The instant he was submerged, Bolan executed a forward semiroll and dived straight down, swimming with arms close to his sides, pedaling hard with both fins. He did not switch on his diving light.

As his eyes became accustomed to the darkness, he detected a faint, wavering illumination from the sky.

Below, he could vaguely make out patterns of pinpoint lights moving about like fireflies on a summer night in Massachusetts.

Bolan swam deeper and deeper away from the filtering rays of the sun. The gloom reached out as if to smother him and increasing pressure tightened around his body.

A school of fish fled at his approach.

He continued angling toward the waving lights in the uneven depths.

A sixth sense alerted him to approaching danger from above and to his left. He rolled sideways as a massive presence glided ominously past him, missing him by inches.

He would have to risk switching on his helmet dive light. He hoped that it would not distract the distant salvage crew from their work around the jumbled shadows of the sunken Liberian freighter.

He activated the light just in time to see the great white shark turn around in a graceful curve before coming at him again.

Bolan rolled and kicked. He registered a momentary impression of the razor-sharp serrated teeth ringing the shark's big mouth.

Then the killer beast was past a second time.

Bolan floated, immobile.

The shark banked again at a distance of some twenty-five meters, then came in for another head-on swipe at this unexpected meal.

Bolan did not want to use the shark gun's bullets to stop the creature. He would need the underwater rounds when he confronted the terrorist frogmen below.

He triggered the gun's electrical mode when the great white was a half meter off, its long, ugly head homing in on Bolan's midsection.

The high-voltage charge stunned the massive beast. It became twenty-eight feet of senseless meat.

Bolan moved in and finished the job with his knife.

This man-eater could not be left around to recover and screw up the mission later on. And the shark's corpse would distract others of the species who could be infesting the vicinity.

Hoping like hell that he had seen the last of deep-sea predators, the Executioner flicked off his helmet light and resumed his descent, moving toward the activity below.

Bolan was gaining on the movement of busy lights when he came across the first ring of the terrorists' defense. Two sentries in full scuba gear, armed with weapons that looked similar to Bolan's shark gun, were drifting slowly. He saw divers stationed as sentries in either direction, barely discernible in the distance.

The leader had established a classic perimeter: evenly spaced teams of divers around the salvage operation. These divers would be in radio contact.

Suddenly Bolan's headset crackled with voices conversing in Spanish. He grinned.

Grimaldi had homed in on the terrorists' frequency and patched it to Bolan.

Bolan's rudimentary grasp of the language told him that either the sentries had no idea of his presence or they were laying a very skillful trap for him.

He took out the two-man team closest to him, swimming up behind one guard and severing the jugular with one knife swipe.

Bolan released the corpse.

The man's body floated upward, trailing the inky cloud spreading into the darkness overhead.

The other guard sensed the commotion and spun around, bringing up his weapon in Bolan's direction.

Bolan stroked the shark gun's trigger and another six-thousand-volt charge zapped living flesh.

The terrorist's body executed a restrained shudder as his hands released the shark gun. Stunned, the diver curled into a fetal position.

The Executioner swam in and finished him with the knife, releasing the body to float upward.

Another sentry team saw the activity and reacted instantly. These two divers split up, tracking their own weapons on Bolan. But they were not fast enough for The Executioner.

Bolan flicked the shark gun to kill mode and triggered a round at the diver on the right before he could warn the others.

Globs of matter shot in all directions as the man's head and helmet exploded.

The guard on Bolan's left brought his weapon to bear and triggered off a round.

But he was not fast enough. The retarding effect of the surrounding water gave Bolan the time he needed.

Bolan kicked himself into a sideways roll.

The bullet missed.

Bolan triggered another round that sent the diver to a watery grave.

Two murky black clouds hung suspended.

Bolan swam in a wide arc, angling well away from the underwater encounter.

There was no way for the rest of the frogman force to accurately detect the source of the exchange between Bolan and the sentries.

Voices in Spanish chattered across the frequency Bolan was monitoring. Then the frequency went blank except for static. That, too, died as Grimaldi realized what had happened and patched Bolan out of their tac net.

The terrorist frogteam was operating under a blanket of radio silence, or they had switched to another frequency.

Bolan realized the team boss would dispatch divers to double-check all the guard points while the salvage operation continued.

They would discover the missing sentries, but the Executioner had already bought the time he needed.

The towering hulk of the sunken freighter was distorted by the filtered glare of underwater high-intensity lamps at the middeck superstructure. The dead ship lay on its side on a ridge amid jagged patches of millepore coral.

The nerve center of the salvage operation appeared to be the cluster of lights. There was a lot of activity. Bolan counted five divers, and he knew there would be more inside the ship.

Bolan swam on, carefully avoiding the sharp coral fingers. At this depth, if he accidentally ripped his suit, he would die instantly. But he was too close now to even consider using his diving light.

He edged closer to the ship's midsection, angling for a ventilator cowl that would offer enough cover for a scan of the area where the illumination seemed to be brightest.

Bolan was halfway to the cowl when he saw, in his peripheral vision, two divers who seemed to materialize out of nowhere. They were approaching Bolan on his right side.

Bolan and the frogmen eyeballed each other simultaneously.

The terrorists stopped swimming, raising their shark guns.

With a powerful kick, Bolan gained the cover of the cowl. He fired the shark gun at the diver closest to him, bursting the man's air tank. The impact tore loose the terrorist's breathing apparatus.

The diver drifted upward wildly amid a burst of bubbles.

The other diver had maneuvered himself behind Bolan. Bolan swung his shark gun around. He triggered an electrical jolt that zapped the diver at the exact instant the man fired his own weapon, pointed well away from Bolan.

The explosion rumbled everywhere. But the concussion would be powerful enough for the terrorist force not to have any doubt that it came from very close.

This underwater hit had suddenly gone very hot.

WHEN HE FELT THE TREMOR of an explosion, Jesus DeSilva swam through the companionway and finned himself to a stop at a point just beyond the shimmering glare of the high-intensity lamps.

He guessed the source of the noise to be one of the underwater weapons supplied by Gurgen, the Russian adviser. But he couldn't pinpoint the direction of the blast.

"Rafael, Santos. Report," demanded DeSilva through the communications system of his diving suit.

No response.

"Everyone, alternate frequency."

The rest of DeSilva's team maintained silence as they activated their DDS transceivers according to the contingency plan.

DeSilva appreciated anew the expert training that

he and his diving team had received outside Cár-
denas, in Cuba, under the careful scrutiny of Com-
rade Gurgen.

The frogteam leader maintained a holding pattern
beyond the cluster of lights near the sideways superstructure of the downed freighter. His finger curled
around his shark gun's trigger. The salvage operation
was suddenly forgotten.

DeSilva glanced at his dive watch. Their air supply
was running dangerously low.

"Luis, Abelardo. Investigate. Be very cautious
now," he ordered two of his divers.

"Be very cautious, my ass," crackled Abelardo's
too cocky voice.

"Maintain silence unless you have something to report," snapped DeSilva, wishing again that he hadn't
been chosen to lead this operation.

The team of terrorist divers were all weary from
being squeezed by seventy-five pounds per square
inch of deep-water pressure.

DeSilva had been supplied with an infrared scanning device for this mission by his Russian adviser.
As he drifted, he surveyed the vicinity with the eight-
inch viewer held close to his face mask.

The IR converted the darkness into a deep twilight
up to a range slightly over 125 feet. At this depth
there were no colors, only various shades of white
and black.

He could see the coral, the sunken freighter.

No sign of anyone.

Suddenly a voice blurted in DeSilva's headset.

"Wait a minute. We see something." It was Luis,
excited exertion obvious in his voice.

"What is your position?" demanded DeSilva.

"He's seen us!" cried Abelardo across the communications frequency. "*Santa Maria!*"

There was no more.

DeSilva felt a clammy sweat form beneath the second skin of his diving suit.

A heartbeat later, he felt another concussion.

DeSilva swam cautiously in the direction of the forward deck. He avoided the lights amidships. He continued to scan the deep with the IR as he propelled himself along.

"Everyone turn off your diving lights," he instructed his team of divers. "Seal off entranceways into the vessel. We've been infiltrated, but we can isolate them. Work together."

Jesus DeSilva had liked nothing about this mission from its inception.

He and his team had diligently searched the passageways of the sunken ship, which were decorated with ghastly, water-rotted corpses of sailors.

And DeSilva's team had not yet found the nuclear device!

The divers had just completed sectoring off another portion of the ship when the rumbling explosions had alerted DeSilva of this penetration.

Jesus DeSilva wondered how many of his men were already dead. He wondered if the mother ship above was attacked.

Who was attacking? he wondered.

The terrorist diver swam on with extreme caution, scanning the murky depths with the IR. He knew he held a slight advantage over whoever was trying to get into this death ship.

DeSilva's antagonists would not be carrying the IR, he knew. Such instruments were bulky and would hinder the swiftness of their attack.

Yet there was no sign of diving lights since he had ordered his men to black out.

Then he realized the penetrators were attacking blind, relying on the high-intensity lamps to guide them!

DeSilva curtly ordered the lights extinguished. The undersea world became black as pitch.

DeSilva grinned to himself.

Now the attackers would be easy marks for him, with the infrared scanner.

It was time to kill or die.

3

Grimaldi held the big Harrier at a sustained hover thirty feet above the choppy ocean where Mack Bolan had disappeared, almost a half hour before.

The pilot tried to ignore a nagging worry that plagued him.

He and Bolan had survived plenty of action together, on lots of hot missions in both Bolan's old Mafia war and in the Executioner's hits out of Stony Man. He had seen the Mafia-busting Bolan "die," then to be reborn as Colonel John Phoenix, under full White House sanction.

Yet through all those battles, the man born Mack Samuel Bolan had never changed.

No way.

Grimaldi knew the blitzing guy better than just about anyone, maybe even better than April Rose, because Jack had seen so much more of the real, unleashed fury of this incredible fighter. Shared combat forged strong bonds of friendship.

The pilot had faith in the big warrior's ability underwater.

But the ace flier had sensed that something was troubling Mack. Grimaldi had seen it plain enough before the communications screwup with the Farm.

He had noticed it during their last mission, too. Of course Bolan was too much of a pro to let it affect his performance. When he fought, he fought. But something was on Bolan's mind.

The pilot was hoping like hell that it would not interfere with this mission.

What the hell was going on with Stony Man?

Where the hell was Phoenix Force?

And all Grimaldi could do was wait, bucking the rowdy air currents of the Atlantic.

He kept trying to reach Stony Man Farm on the radio, alternating the mission red priority frequencies.

Nothing.

Grimaldi itched for action.

He got it.

Three beeps appeared on the radar-scan map console, approaching rapidly from the southeast.

Grimaldi tried to establish radio contact.

There was no response.

Those three fast-approaching beeps could be Phoenix Force, but Grimaldi quickly dismissed that thought.

Phoenix Force was scrambling to this rendezvous at sea from their last Stony Man assignment. Since the five-man combat team was heading here from one point, it didn't make sense to Jack Grimaldi that they would split up in transit. But he couldn't be sure until visual contact was made.

Grimaldi bristled in the Harrier's cockpit.

Phoenix Force should have responded to Grimaldi's attempt at radio contact, but there was the communications foul-up with Stony Man to consider. It might somehow be affecting a linkup between Grimaldi and Phoenix Force.

Three choppers suddenly emerged from the low thunderheads.

Grimaldi's doubts were confirmed as they immediately opened fire on the Harrier.

He was ready for it. He tugged the jet fighter into a sharp evasive maneuver the instant he recognized gunflashes from the three approaching aircraft. He heard a line of bullets thud into his plane's body somewhere behind him.

Grimaldi recognized the approaching gunships as Cobras, probably surplus from the Vietnam War.

They'd been hanging back beyond the Harrier's radar range and were probably carrying replacements for the divers Bolan was now fighting underwater.

The Cobras were equipped with rockets, 40mm cannons and miniguns.

Grimaldi left the hammering of those weapons far behind. The best chopper pilot alive was no match for the Harrier's jet-action capabilities. The Stony pilot could easily have outrun the three helicopters, but he could not desert the area in case Mack surfaced. He had to get the Cobras away from there somehow.

The Harrier screamed into a hard fast bank. He faced the enemy.

The three choppers started to break formation, fanning out to opposite sides. The Cobra in the middle was sailing in to engage the Harrier. The chopper's miniguns blazed twin streams of lead tracers that sailed wide of Grimaldi's plane.

Grimaldi triggered a sidewinding heatseeker that blasted the approaching enemy copter. The chopper exploded into a fireball before plummeting into the ocean.

One down, two to go.

Goddamn, Phoenix Force, where are you? Grimaldi wondered.

He arced the big bird back from the four streams of upcoming fire and rockets from the two remaining aircraft.

Grimaldi caught himself shredding his lower lip between his teeth. *If they get me, Bolan will be dead when he shows his head above water.*

It was time to face the two wild Cobras.

But the two gunships had maneuvered themselves for a run at the Harrier from two directions. Even the mighty Harrier could only take on one of them at a time.

Grimaldi prayed for the best and sent 30mm zingers at the chopper nearest him.

The thundering explosion of the hit cut through the roar of the Harrier as another Cobra disintegrated into a ball of flame.

The Stony pilot shifted his war bird to track on chopper number three.

While the fighter jet's cannon had been busy canceling the second chopper, Cobra number three had got the Harrier in its sights.

Grimaldi saw it too late. A missile from the Cobra came whistling at the Harrier.

The ace pilot had just begun to tug the responsive jet into an evasive action.

But his luck ran out.

He bit off one last curse. He felt the mighty plane respond to his touch, but not fast enough.

The missile caught the Harrier's tail in a hellfire of sound and fury.

For Jack Grimaldi, everything went black.

MACK BOLAN MADE AN ALLY of the ocean's dark floor in the same way he would befriend the night on any other hit.

The Executioner swam through the gloomy depths ten meters off the bow of the sunken vessel.

He saw the enemy divers douse their dive lights.

In the illumination of the underwater lamps amidships, he saw the terrorist force breaking up, merging with the deeper shadows of the ship.

Bolan sensed movement to his left. He bent his body backward and swam away.

He registered a momentary glimpse of an approaching diver, holding what looked like an infrared scanning device.

This would be the team leader, Bolan knew. They would not all be entrusted with costly IRs.

The high-intensity lights were extinguished.

The frogman leader did not see his enemy.

Bolan propelled himself faster, gauging the approximate position where he had last seen the diver with the IR.

In the darkness, it was impossible to know for sure.

The deep-sea pressure made every move slower, more laborious.

Bolan unsheathed his knife, then risked switching on his dive light for one second to confirm that he had homed in on his target.

The terrorist frogman could not turn around in time to react.

Bolan plunged the blade into Jesus DeSilva's throat. The thrust severed the terrorist's breathing system.

The man's body thrashed for an instant then hung suspended as a dark cloud spread upward.

The IR scanner tumbled into Bolan's grip.

He used the infrared device to advantage to take out two more divers.

Bolan entered the ship and swam on through the maze of corridors, guiding himself with the IR, searching.

He came upon the body of a trapped seaman, the ghastly corpse already half devoured by fish.

There was no sign of sharks now.

He swam on, pedaling his way the length of the sunken wreck.

He glanced at his watch. Only ten minutes of air time left. He had to find that nuclear device. He considered radio contact with Grimaldi, but decided against it. He still did not know how many men were left. They were around him in the gloom of this sunken ship. He could feel it. They would be listening.

Bolan continued his search, thinking about his air supply.

He was running out of places to look for the nuclear device.

He found it in the middle of a row of three nondescript lockers: a suitcase-sized container with the markings Bolan was looking for.

And with it, Bolan found them.

The underwater compartment blazed to life with a high-noon glare that pinned Bolan in its center.

These divers had split off from the others and found the cargo they were looking for. Then they waited for the invader to swim his way into the killground.

Bolan twisted sideways as weapons began to rumble, spitting projectiles where he had been an instant before.

He unleashed a round from his shark gun that took out the lamp and pitched the killzone into total darkness.

He had been forced to drop the infrared device. The Executioner fired off a close pattern of heavy slugs from his weapon, aiming from memory at the positions of three divers before the lights went off.

He waited for a few moments and no one challenged him.

He chanced a quick scan with his diver light on. He found and retrieved the IR.

He flicked the infrared device upward and gazed through it. He saw three floating corpses, trapped from rising any farther by the walls of the compartment. The water around the divers took on a deeper hue in the IR viewer.

Bolan returned his attention to the nuclear device.

There were two handles on the container. He gripped one handle and began swimming away from the underwater killzone, holding the scanner up before him as he retraced his route.

He wondered if the damn thing would be intact. Or had these men all died for nothing. No. Nothing is ever for nothing.

The dead divers had consciously chosen this path. But they had been brought unwittingly to this appointment with their executioner. Whether they were motivated by greed or power, Bolan could not know. But it did not matter now. Their evil deeds had culminated in a fitting demise in the hellish depths of the dark Atlantic.

Now the bastards were shark food.

All that remained for Bolan was withdrawal.

Gripping the container, he swam on.

The underwater warrior conserved the remaining air in his tanks, breathing shallowly despite his effort.

He turned on the diving light and began to swim clear of the dead ship.

He ran into no further opposition as he moved upward.

Bolan released the IR and stroked faster toward the surface with the deadly cargo.

It was time to alert Grimaldi, up in the Harrier, to get ready for him. He would have to spend time in the decompression chamber on the boat then a quick flight back to the States. The communications blackout with Stony Man still troubled him.

"Stony Man One to Stony Bird. I'm coming up, Jack. I've got it. Do you read me?"

No response.

Bolan was about to try to raise Grimaldi again when the watery world around him thumped with a loud, hollow sound.

Bolan looked up.

And saw Death descending.

The massive shape of Grimaldi's Harrier was coming toward him.

Its misshapen hulk was sinking like an oversized stone, plunging directly at Bolan.

4

Bolan did not try to swim out from under the fast-descending tonnage of the Harrier.

He reversed his course and dived back down the way he had come. He gained cover within the sunken hulk of the Liberian freighter.

He made it with one heartbeat to spare, still gripping the nuclear device.

The tips of his fins cleared the entranceway to the tilted superstructure of the ship just as the heavy weight of the Harrier impacted the submerged vessel. Bolan was socked by the nearest wall of the companionway as the ship jarred.

He reversed himself and swam out of the companionway to find the Harrier lodged against the superstructure and the ocean floor.

The downed fighter plane was still making strange little underwater sounds as it settled into its new environment. The Harrier had sustained a serious hit to its tail section.

Bolan's gut constricted with apprehension.

Grimaldi!

He approached the plane with extreme caution despite his concern for Jack. He raised the shark gun, which was slung around his shoulder by its strap. He now scanned the vicinity of the wreckage for terrorist divers he might have missed.

There was no one.

Bolan found no sign of Grimaldi in or around the Harrier's cockpit. The pilot was not strapped into his seat. Jack had not sunk with the plane.

The tanks strapped to Bolan's back were almost empty. Any more time spent down there would be suicide.

Once more Bolan began to swim toward the surface, the shark gun again strapped across his back. Using his free arm and both fins, he propelled himself up and away from the ship toward the first glimmer of dull sunlight that drew closer and closer overhead.

Bolan broke the surface on the swell of a cresting wave. He bobbed like a cork on the endless expanse of rough ocean. His face mask cleared water, and he looked around to get his bearings.

There was no sign of Jack.

A jet turbine Bell chopper, boasting 5.56mm miniguns and 40mm cannons mounted externally on turrets, hovered clearly against the low grim cloud ceiling.

A cable hung from the open door of the Huey. The cable was pulled taut by the weight of Jack Grimaldi, who was being winched up toward the aircraft.

Bolan could make out four members of Phoenix Force crowded in the side opening of the Huey: Gary Manning, the Canadian explosives expert; Keio Ohara, the Japanese martial-arts master; David McCarter, the British brawler; and Rafael Encizo, the Cuban underwater demolitions specialist.

That meant it was Yakov Katzenelenbogen, the Israeli-French intelligence vet, topkick of Phoenix Force, who was flying the chopper.

Bolan glimpsed the smoldering debris of what had been another helicopter on the surface of the water. The wreckage was slowly disappearing into the hungry rolling waves.

The boat that marked the site of the terrorist salvage operation bobbed on the stormy Atlantic.

Bolan knew he would need decompression time aboard that boat.

He saw the men of Phoenix hoist a very wet Grimaldi into the safety of their gunship.

Bolan lifted a victorious thumbs-up sign to the guys.

He punched into the tac net as he swam.

"Is that you, Yakov?"

"You were expecting Jacques Cousteau?" grumbled the Phoenix Force honcho from behind the chopper controls. "Get yourself onto that boat and into decompression, Striker. Then we talk."

Bolan fought the sea toward the boat and the DC. He tugged along the nuclear device that had gotten so many men killed this day.

There were still too many things left unexplained. They chewed at him inside, demanding action. Like a communications screwup that could only mean more trouble....

"Yeah," Bolan replied grimly as he swam toward the wind-tossed boat on the rough sea. "Then we talk."

ONE HOUR LATER, Jack Grimaldi was still wearing the widest ear-to-ear grin that Bolan had ever seen.

"Man, I'm here to tell you," the ace pilot was telling Bolan and Yakov, "I must've aged ten years in the ten seconds it took those terrorist bastards to shoot me into the drink. I was never so glad to see one of these big Hueys coming to the rescue. Not even in Nam."

Grimaldi was now at the controls of the Huey.

The helicopter was in the same stationary hold it had maintained while Bolan did his time in decompression.

Then Colonel Phoenix was pulled aboard the chopper by the same winch that had rescued Grimaldi from an Atlantic death.

Two vessels now rode the ocean beneath the Huey. The terrorists' boat had been joined by another trawler while Bolan was in DC; a trawler that was in fact a well-disguised U.S. spy boat sailing with computerized eavesdropping capability and armed with torpedoes and missiles.

The spy ship had been ordered from its regular course for this "accidental" rendezvous with the chopper.

"After all the times you've airlifted this guy out of hotspots," said Katz to Grimaldi, with a nod to indicate Bolan, "I'd say you've damn well earned yourself some luck, my friend. It was our pleasure, Jack."

"Where are the others?" Bolan asked Katz.

He was referring to the other members of Phoenix Force. They were not aboard the Huey.

Katz pointed down at the raging sea.

"Rafael is supervising the cleanup inside the

sunken ship,'' the Phoenix Force leader told the Executioner. ''It's ours in accordance with open-sea salvage regulations.''

Bolan fired a cigarette. He felt good to be above water again.

''Any idea where those Cobras were from?'' he asked Katz.

Katzenelenbogen shook his head.

''The spy trawler down below has a far wider radar range than this Huey, or the Harrier Jack was flying.''

''Don't remind me,'' groused Jack from behind the Huey's controls. ''I feel terrible losing that plane.''

''Like hell, Jack,'' said Bolan. ''You did everything you could. You nailed two of them before they hit you.'' He nodded to the nuclear device at their feet. ''And this mission is a success.'' He looked again at Katz. ''What did the trawler's radar turn up?''

''A few maybes. The choppers could have come from a modified trawler like the ones below, fixed to handle the salvage crew and the choppers to ferry them around without drawing attention to the actual site. No way to check them out, though, unless you want to take the time now.''

Bolan grimaced.

''Damn. I'd like to. But this device has got to be delivered. And there's that other thing.''

Katz stared down at the nuclear bomb.

The hell bomb was still sealed in its innocent-appearing suitcase disguise.

"Hard to believe that something so inconspicuous could be worth so much killing."

"Keio might be the only one among us who can truly appreciate the horror of this little baby," said Bolan. "He lost members of his family at Nagasaki."

"That's what makes Keio so intent on these missions," Yakov said, nodding. "He reminds us all that what happened before must never happen again."

"Set a course for home, Jack." Bolan turned to the Phoenix Force leader. "We'll lower you now, Yakov. Thanks for flying-in this Huey."

Katzenelenbogen shrugged off the thanks. He moved toward the open doorway, to the winched pulley rope.

"This helicopter is modified with auxiliary fuel tanks, Striker. You'll make it to that carrier for refueling easy enough. There's a jet waiting outside Miami to take you back to Stony Man."

Then Katz got a grip on the thick rope.

"The trawler will see you away when you're done here," said Bolan. "Others besides those terrorists will be on their way here soon, Katz."

"Like the European end of the deal?" asked Katz. "Able Team is working that angle right now. They could have something on it already. And there could be something more than a bomb aboard that sunken freighter. Rafael has them going over the captain's quarters, Striker. The safe, that kind of thing. If there's anything salvageable down there that we can use from an intel standpoint, we'll bring it home with us."

"See you at Stony Man, then. Good luck," said Bolan.

He activated the winch.

It began lowering Katz toward the U.S. spy ship below.

"Mack, find out what the hell went wrong on that communications blackout."

"I intend to," said the big blitzer grimly. "That's a promise."

When the Phoenix Force team boss was aboard the deck of the U.S. trawler, Bolan slammed shut the door and shouted to Grimaldi above the constant, high-pitched whine of the chopper.

"Home, Jack."

"You know it, bossman," said the flyboy, grinning.

The pilot eased them away from the site with a gentle increase of power. The bobbing trawlers became specks on the choppy Atlantic. The Huey lifted off into the gray sky in a northwesterly course for home.

America.

The U.S. of A.

A place Mack Bolan was seeing less and less of these days.

What would he find waiting for him at Stony Man?

The mission was successful. There were no casualties for the Stony Man soldiers and the hell-bomb device, whether it survived the ship's sinking intact or not, was on its way to the proper authorities.

Any other time, Bolan's pulse would have slowed down by now from the adrenaline rush of that underwater action. Now he thought of home and those good people who shared the burden of these terrorist wars every step of the way: Hal, Kurtzman, Konzaki. And of course his lady, April, who made the wheels turn and was always there for Bolan with a candle in the window.

Stony Man.

Right.

Everything this big warrior held near and dear.

His thoughts were on these people now, sure. But it was not the warmth of a reunion to be anticipated. It was the nagging concern he had felt since they had first lost connection with Stony Man prior to the undersea hit.

Bolan's adrenaline was still pumping.

The spy trawler's computers had their own satellite linkup. An operator aboard ship had worked on the problem while Bolan was in decompression. When a connection with Stony Man Farm was finally achieved it was via a communications patch into an unscrambled phone line at the Stony Man command center.

Bolan spoke briefly with Hal Brognola. The head Fed did not mince words or tip anything that would breach security.

Hal spoke seven words over the staticky connection, saying nothing to ease Bolan's concern or slow the adrenaline down.

"Come home, Striker. ASAP. There's big trouble."

5

Andrzej Konzaki was in a coma.

The Stony Man armorer lay struggling for life in the emergency sick bay of Stony Man Farm. Mack Bolan and April Rose stood next to an armed man in uniform on the other side of an observation window in the hospital facility.

Konzaki was enshrouded in an oxygen tent. Tubes ran to him from two bottles.

A nurse beside the bed monitored a cardiograph machine that registered a very weak pulse.

The tough-looking man in uniform who stood next to Bolan was Captain Wade. He was in charge of the security force that patrolled the perimeter of Stony Man Farm.

"He was reported missing at 1400 hours, sir," Wade reported. "We instituted a search immediately."

All Farm personnel made voice contact with one of Kurtzman's central computers every two hours. A security precaution.

"Was he missing before or after the explosion?" asked Bolan.

"Before, sir."

April spoke up.

"Why do you think Konzaki wasn't killed, Mack?"

"Being in a wheelchair probably saved Konzaki's life," growled Bolan. "At least, so far."

Wade picked up the thought.

"The angle of the blow. Sure. Whoever slugged him wasn't used to chopping down at that angle. The blow that meant to kill Mr. Konzaki caught him at the wrong angle."

April's lovely features were taut with an inner rage she could not conceal.

"A man in a wheelchair...."

"Do you have anything else to report, Captain?" Bolan asked Wade.

"No, sir, I'm afraid not. No signs of penetration anywhere along the perimeter. The ground is soft this time of year. But there were no signs of footprints where Mr. Konzaki was attacked."

Bolan had heard enough. He could do no good for Konzaki standing there.

"Captain Wade, return to your men. April, let's see what Kurtzman has for us."

It was twenty minutes after Grimaldi had set them down on the Stony Man airstrip in the F-14 Tomcat jet that had flown them to Washington from Miami.

At this moment, the pilot was at the airstrip's camouflaged hangar, ensuring that the jet would be ready if needed on short notice.

The brain center of the Farm was a sprawling collection of rustic buildings set amid a dense forest of hardwood and conifer and the occasional grassy meadow like the one that surrounded the ordinary-looking "farm buildings."

In fact, the buildings and the underground facility beneath them housed the brightly lit, modern headquarters of the Executioner's Phoenix world.

The Blue Ridge terrain was dominated on the far horizon by Stony Man Mountain, one of the highest peaks in the region.

The weather was unseasonably warm, but the mountain was wreathed in low-hanging clouds that gave the spring day a grim, foreboding look.

Bolan felt the same way inside.

He had known Andrzej Konzaki only by the man's work in the Stony Man program. In that regard, Bolan ranked the Farm's armorer at the absolute top, and he now regretted not having gotten to know Konzaki better.

Konzaki was officially with the Special Weapons Development branch of the CIA, unofficially attached to Stony Man shortly after the inception of the Phoenix program. Konzaki, legless since Vietnam, was one of the most innovative armorers in the world, a master weaponsmith. His CIA profile read: "trust him."

Konzaki had never let Bolan down.

And now the guy lay in a coma with a less than fifty-fifty chance of pulling through. With the identity of his assailant locked up inside where it would stay forever if a good man named Konzaki died.

Aaron Kurtzman was waiting for Bolan and April at the polished conference table in the briefing room, down the corridor from where Andrzej Konzaki lay.

"All of our computer-satellite linkups are totaled," grumbled The Bear. "Someone got inside the terminal housing at the back of this building. My guess is they used some form of plastique."

"How long to repair?" asked Bolan.

"The necessary component replacements are on their way," Kurtzman reported, "but it's still taking time, too much damn time, because Stony Man Farm supposedly does not exist. For that same reason we can't go through any of the standard channels."

Bolan stood up and began to pace about the briefing room as he put the thing together aloud. An urge for action had him restless.

"Wade's men didn't find any signs of penetration. That could mean there was no penetration."

April frowned.

"An inside job? That's...almost unthinkable, Mack. Everyone at the Farm has been screened so thoroughly."

"Determine the key people in this area and screen them again," said Bolan. "Start with Captain Wade."

"As you say," agreed April.

"What about the saboteur?" asked Kurtzman thoughtfully. "Whether the damage was done by a man or woman inside the Farm or by infiltration, we still don't have any point to start from."

"We narrow it to categories," said Bolan. "Someone has tried to sabotage our operation. Is our enemy domestic or foreign? How did they learn about us? Bear, I want you to backtrack over every possible security leak point you can think of in the program.''

"Roger.''

"I ordered Wade to double his security force as soon as Konzaki was reported missing,'' said April.

"Good work,'' said Bolan. "Now triple it. And I'll want to review the defense with you and Wade after it's been revised.''

"Defense?'' echoed Kurtzman. "Sounds as if you expect an attack.''

"That sabotage was a soft probe to test our reflexes,'' said Bolan. "And I'd say everyone here reflexed right on the money.''

"That means,'' added April, "that if someone is planning to attack the Farm, they'll hit us with a sizable force.'' She stood, tall, lush-bodied.

"When they hit, we damn well better be ready for them,'' she said. "I'd better get on it.''

There had to be time for that one brief brush of lips against his cheek. Her nearness always tantalized Bolan.

Then she was gone.

Dear April. So damn efficient.

"What's the status on Able Team?'' Bolan asked Kurtzman. "Yakov told me they were homed in on the European end of that terrorist deal I just squashed.''

"Lyons, Blancanales and Schwarz are poised to strike at the headquarters of a man they've identified only as 'The Dragon.' The Dragon runs his show from a mountain fortress in the Hindu Kush, almost inaccessible except by helicopter.''

"The Himalayas," Bolan commented. "Fourteen-thousand-foot mountains between Pakistan and Afghanistan. A smugglers' route for thousands of years."

"The Dragon is the biggest broker we've been able to identify," said Kurtzman. "If we stop him, we could practically dry up the flow of arms to all the terrorist groups. And maybe give us the next link in the chain to who pulls the big strings."

Sure. Bolan knew well. Anyone who thought that the various terrorist groups functioned solely on empty rhetoric simply did not know the truth. Activities such as kidnapping, extortion and robbery netted millions of dollars per year for those unknowns who bathed in the blood of innocent victims.

And now the men of Mack Bolan's Able Team were halfway around the world, ready to make one of the biggest hits of all in this new war against terrorism. Dry up their arms supply.

Able Team was a three-man unit: Carl Lyons, a former LAPD cop who'd been a Bolan ally since the early days of the Executioner's former Mafia war, Rosario "Pol" Blancanales and Hermann "Gadgets" Schwarz, two more combat specialists who had shared the hellground experience with Mack Bolan as part of the Executioner's Able Penetration Team in that long-ago war.

Three exceptional fighting men.

Yeah.

Three men.

Against who the hell knew what?

The Dragon was a new one to Bolan.

He voiced a thought that had been with him since his arrival at the Farm.

"Where's Hal?"

A phone at Kurtzman's elbow buzzed.

Kurtzman picked up the receiver, listened, then extended the phone to Bolan. "You want him, you got him. Mr. Liaison himself."

Bolan took the receiver.

"Hal?"

"Welcome home, Striker."

"Where are you, Hal? You should be here."

"Would you believe the White House?" said Brognola.

"And what's cooking at the Man's place?"

"We're waiting on Colonel John Phoenix."

"We?"

"The president, Striker. And a guy named Lee Farnsworth."

"And what are we waiting on Colonel Phoenix for?" asked Bolan.

There was a pause, as if Brognola did not want to reply.

"Farnsworth wants the president to disband the Stony Man operation."

"What?"

"You know who Farnsworth is?"

"CFB."

"Right. The Central Foreign Bureau. He says we've stepped on CFB's toes with one of our operations. Got two of their men killed. He claims it's happened before."

"Hal, is my presence there absolutely necessary? The blackout tonight could've been a probe for something else."

"You cannot stand up the Man, Striker."

"The president's a man of good judgment," said Bolan.

"But Farnsworth has his ear, and he's making a strong case against us," insisted Hal. "I hate to remind you, old buddy, but you are a team player, remember? Your one-man-war days are over."

"I wonder, Hal. I'm starting to get an itch."

"Dammit, we are talking about the goddamn president, Striker."

"You're right, Hal. He is the boss. I don't like it, but I'll be there in fifteen minutes."

APRIL MET HIM near the helicopter takeoff pad.

The clouds over the mountains were moving in.

A warm breeze played with loose tendrils of her shoulder-length hair and its warm gold highlights. Movie-star hair.

The concerned look in April's eyes was that of a lover who cares about her man.

Bolan noticed one difference about the lady since he had last seen her in the briefing room awhile ago.

April wore a .44 Magnum with a six-inch barrel in a fast-draw holster on her shapely right hip. She was also carrying a spare gun-holster rig.

The lady handled weapons like a carpenter handled a saw.

But still beautiful, yeah.

No one ever said that tough and competent could not be synonymous with feminine, thought Bolan, and the woman who gave him her heart was damn well proof of that.

Bolan gestured to the spare rig and weapon that she carried over her shoulder.

"For Aaron," she explained. "It looks like he and I might be doing more than sitting on the sidelines this time."

The president could wait.

Bolan grabbed April Rose with one arm and pulled her to him.

She came willingly, pressing herself against the big man with a kiss that was all passion, all love and fire.

"God speed you back to me, Colonel Thunder," she whispered fiercely in his ear when they were close.

Another kiss.

Then it was time to move out.

Bolan boarded the chopper. But the urge to remain at Stony Man Farm pulled at him stronger than ever.

Someone had breached Stony Man Farm's security.

And there was Konzaki.

Bolan sensed that the lives of all his Stony Man allies were already on the line.

But Hal was right.

You do not turn down a request from the Man.

Bolan was airlifted from Stony Man Farm knowing that there would be no room for miscalculation or fumbling on this coming night that was about to cloak the nation's capital.

It was a jungle out there, Washington, D.C., or no.

And the Executioner was back in town.

6

The familiar low skyline of D.C. was bathed in dusk as Grimaldi piloted the bubble-front Hughes helicopter with Mack Bolan aboard.

No city in America is more drenched in history and legend than Washington.

Bolan knew this city, and he knew something of its history.

This land had been a blazed hellground. The British captured and sacked the city in 1814. It wasn't until the twentieth century that Washington was transformed from an unkempt village into the city of today: a hellground of another kind.

Wonderland on the Potomac, Hal called it.

With the reality of the ghetto only a stone's throw from the power brokers who steered the course of the nation, the city was a study in contrasts. The Washington Monument obelisk, the Lincoln Memorial and the Jefferson Memorial, shrines to the visionaries of equality, were set against some of the worst poverty Bolan had ever seen.

Bolan wore a two-piece suit of subdued blue and a sky-blue shirt and red tie for his meeting with the president.

On his left shoulder, under the suit jacket, the

Beretta 93-R pistol nestled in a concealed shoulder speed rig.

Bolan's Beretta had been modified with a new sound suppressor and a flash-hider for night firing. The gun was designed for fast killing. Konzaki had devised a forehand grip that folded down to provide controlled two-handed firing. The 93-R saw action on nearly every Bolan mission.

Another debt to Konzaki.

He also toted a black leather briefcase that contained additional items he liked to have close at hand, including Big Thunder, the impressive stainless-steel .44 AutoMag.

The chopper began descending.

"Coming in," called Grimaldi above the steady throbbing of the rotor.

If Grimaldi felt exhausted, as he had to be, he wasn't showing it. Bolan at least had caught some shut-eye on the flight to Stony Man from down south.

The eighteen acres of White House grounds were a maze of lengthening shadows on the south side of Pennsylvania Avenue. Grimaldi touched down smoothly on a grassy area in back of the executive mansion.

The White House.

More living history.

The British had razed it in 1814 and when the present three-story structure of simple, stately design was rebuilt, the scorched Virginia freestone of the home of every president since Adams had been painted over a stark white, and it had been the White House ever since.

Bolan dropped from the chopper's door before the chopper even settled. The Executioner left his briefcase with the pilot.

History is being made right now, thought Bolan as he hustled at a slow jog from beneath the whirling blades of the helicopter. The Phoenix program spanned more than one administration, but combat specialist John Phoenix had never been called to this house.

Grimaldi cut the chopper's engine and waited.

Bolan approached three husky guys clad almost identically in conservative suits. They met him near an entrance to the building. Bolan made two of these White House staffers as armed Secret Service agents.

"This way, Colonel, please," said the third man.

They escorted Bolan into a hallway of sedate oak paneling and thick red carpet.

Hal Brognola and another man, whom Bolan recognized as Farnsworth, the CFB chief, stood waiting a few paces to the side of the closed heavy oak door of the Oval Office, the president's inner sanctum.

The two Secret Service agents fell back. The other staffer strode to the door of the president's office, knocked politely, then opened the door and stuck his head inside.

Brognola's permanently five-o'clock-shadowed face wore a tight glower that only barely brightened when he saw Bolan.

Stony Man's gruff White House liaison greeted Bolan with a firm handshake.

"Colonel Phoenix, thanks for getting here so fast." Hal introduced the man standing beside him. "This is Lee Farnsworth, Central Foreign Bureau."

Farnsworth was a strapping, blond-haired man in his early forties who had the physical conditioning of a man twenty years younger. Sharp eyes that had seen it all were set in a serious, granite face.

Bolan considered what he knew about the guy and the operation he headed.

The CFB was the Defense Department's special unit for intelligence-gathering and covert operations. It was set up to supplement the CIA and the Defense Intelligence Agency. The Pentagon intended the unit to operate around the world.

Bolan knew that the agency had been formed in 1980 during the planning of the raid to free the American hostages in Iran when the Pentagon was dissatisfied with the intelligence data it was getting from the CIA.

Much like the Phoenix operation, the CFB conducted clandestine operations without "presidential finding," the legal authorization required by Congress. Bolan also knew that the Senate and House Intelligence committees had not been advised of the unit's existence, as required by law.

The CIA and the Defense Intelligence Agency, which is the Pentagon's regular intelligence unit, were unaware of the CFB's activities.

The bureau had deployed personnel around the world using false identification to collect intelligence.

Bolan respected Lee Farnsworth and what his

agency had accomplished. He knew of at least one coup stage-managed by the CFB in which the U.S. had gained a new ally where one was badly needed.

If Farnsworth's estimation of Phoenix was mutual, he did nothing to show it. He glanced away as if Bolan was not there.

The White House staffer stepped into the hallway from the Oval Office and approached the waiting three.

"The president will see you now, gentlemen."

The two Secret Service men intercepted them at the office door. One of the Feds held a metal-detector device that beeped when he fanned Bolan with it.

"We check all our weapons or the meeting's off," clipped Farnsworth.

"Strict security regulation to protect the Man," Brognola said to Bolan. "Lee and I have already turned ours over."

Bolan didn't like it, but he handed over the Beretta. Then he, Farnsworth and Brognola stepped into the president's tomb of an office where heavy drapes were drawn against the day's last light.

The door closed behind them, leaving them in private with the man who strode forward to greet them.

Bolan had never met any of the presidents he had served under as Colonel John Phoenix. A good soldier must remain apolitical, was Bolan's philosophy.

The president shook hands with each man in turn. Up close, the chief executive showed a strain not discernible in the media pictures Bolan had seen. The president looked tired and edgy.

"You have my word, gentlemen, that this meeting is strictly off the record, any record," the Man told them. "This meeting has never taken place. I'm in Louisville, and you are not here. Please be seated. Let us attend to this business as expediently as possible."

The four men seated themselves in a loose circle of wing chairs just off from the president's desk.

"Mr. President," began Lee Farnsworth, "Stony Man has screwed up a mission that the CFB spent over a year setting up. It's happened before, too."

"Let's have specifics," growled Brognola. "What mission of yours have we supposedly screwed up?"

"The Dragon," said Farnsworth.

The president glanced at Hal and Bolan.

"Is this true, gentlemen? I'm familiar with The Dragon file. Has Stony Man become involved?"

Hal looked itchy to light one of his cigars, but it was widely known that the president was a reformed smoker.

"We do have a three-man combat unit called Able Team that is working The Dragon angle," Hal admitted.

"The Atlantic thing," put in Farnsworth. "That was another angle of it."

"So it came together from different sides," gruffed Brognola. "If Able Team get their hands on The Dragon, it saves CFB the work."

"The Dragon is not the top man in his corner of the world," groused the CFB boss. "He has a partner. You didn't know that because it was our men who developed the intel. The Dragon runs the enforcement arm of the organization. The partner carries the list of names of backers and associates around in his or her head. This partner will sacrifice The Dragon if he has to. It's important to our mission that The Dragon's partner not have any idea that we have a mole inside his organization.''

"Get back to Able Team," said Brognola.

"If Able Team had been allowed to hit The Dragon's fortress, the CFB would have risked the operation and the life of the contact we have inside.''

"You're speaking of Able Team in the past tense," said Bolan, with a sinking feeling.

"Our man next to The Dragon blew the whistle," Farnsworth said smugly. "The Dragon has been alerted. He's already lit out from that fort of his.''

"At least you alerted Able Team," said Hal, but the words came out a question.

"Stony Man has stepped on our toes often enough to need a lesson," growled Farnsworth. "Your men of Able Team are the lesson." He turned to the president. "Sir, we lost two men in Morocco last year because Stony Man operated in the area without CFB clearance. It happened the year before that to an agent in El Salvador.''

Bolan felt his fury rising. He slowly got to his feet and felt the eyes of the others following him.

"Are you telling me that you've left our men in those mountains to be slaughtered?''

Bolan hardly recognized his own voice.

"This happens because the CFB and Stony Man

are two completely different types of operations trying to do the same job in the same territory,'' rasped Farnsworth.

The president frowned.

"Dammit, Lee, sometimes you go too damn far."

"My operatives are trained in the art of espionage," Farnsworth insisted. "Their training is rooted in accomplishing a mission without making waves. That's the spy business. These Stony Man, uh, 'combat specialists,' tramp through our well-set-up operations like goddamn bulls through a china shop. I submit, Mr. President, that the Stony Man project is crippling us from within. The Phoenix unit should be disbanded."

"Deal me out if you want to," said Bolan softly. "That suits this soldier just fine."

Brognola stood to face Bolan.

"Striker, don't—"

"Please, Colonel, you must understand," said the president in a reasonable tone to Bolan. "I share with my predecessors the view that Stony Man is vital to our national security. Don't you gentlemen feel there is some way for both your units to coexist?"

Bolan turned to the president.

"What does General Crawford say about this?"

Perhaps the driving force in the development of Stony Man, and one of the main reasons Bolan had decided to take on the proffered government-sanctioned job at the end of his Mafia wars, was now-retired Brigadier General James Crawford. He had been Mack Bolan's commanding officer in Vietnam and had been invaluable in making the Phoenix dream a reality.

"As you know, General Crawford oversaw the creation of Stony Man and the CFB," said the president. "Like myself, the general hopes a compromise can be worked out."

Bolan faced the president head-on.

"It will have to wait, sir. I'm needed in the field tonight. You've been briefed on what happened at Stony Man?"

"I have."

"Then you'll understand why I can't spend the night sitting here talking policy. Will that be all, sir?"

A good-natured glint came into the president's eye.

"Yes, Colonel. Thank you for coming. We'll be in touch."

Bolan was in the outer hallway again, slipping on his retrieved shoulder rig, when Hal Brognola caught up with him.

The burly Fed wore a mixed expression of awe and frustration.

"You are the damndest guy," was all Hal could muster.

Bolan stalked outside into the night. Brognola kept pace with him.

"What was that business on the phone about an itch?" asked Hal. "And telling the president to deal you out if he wants to? I think we had better have a serious talk, Striker."

"We will, Hal. But not tonight."

"There you go with 'not tonight' again, just like

you told the Man. I want an explanation. I know about the communications blackout at Stony Man Farm. But what makes you so damn sure there's going to be an attack on the Farm *tonight*?''

"I'm not sure, Hal. I'm not going to Stony Man."

Brognola blinked.

"You're not? Where the blazes are you going?''

Bolan glanced at the city of lights beyond the perimeter of the floodlit White House grounds.

"I'm going out there," Bolan told him. "Konzaki is in a coma, hanging on to life by a thread. Three good men are on the other side of the world and need to be alerted and told that they're walking into a trap.''

"You think The Dragon has the place wired?''

Bolan nodded, his face a grim mask.

"With enough firepower to kill Lyons, Schwarz and Blancanales before they know what hit them. And it's about to happen at any minute now, but we can't get word to them because someone sabotaged Stony Man communications. I am going to find who did this to us, Hal. They are not going to get another chance.''

"But where will you start? You don't have any leads.''

Grimaldi, waiting in the chopper, saw Bolan coming and revved up the engine in preparation for take off.

Bolan raised his voice for Hal to hear.

"I've already started. I'm going to shake this damn town to its roots. I'll get the answers. And it's happening tonight.''

Bolan jogged beneath the whirling blades and climbed into the Hughes.

Brognola watched as Grimaldi smoothly lifted them off. The blinking red lights of the chopper grew smaller and smaller as the Hughes receded into the night sky.

Then Brognola gave in to his urge and reached into a pocket for a cigar.

He paused before lighting it, still looking into the dark sky long after the chopper disappeared.

"You are the damndest guy," he said again to no one.

Brognola pocketed the unlit cigar and walked back into the White House.

7

"Where to?" asked Grimaldi.

The evening lights of Washington and the gridiron arrangement of streets cut by diagonal avenues raced by beneath the chopper's Plexiglas.

"We need an airfield," said Bolan above the steady rumble of the chopper. "I want you on standby alert for the rest of the night."

"Bolling?"

"Not tonight. Make it National. I'll need a car with no government tie-in."

"A rental," said the pilot, glancing at the big warrior beside him. "I've seen you like this before, soldier. You're on the kill. And it's a lone-wolf play, just like it used to be."

Bolan's eyes were chips of ice.

"Patch me through to Stony Man."

Local communications were relayed through a government scrambler frequency.

Kurtzman wasted no time on amenities when the connection was made.

"I have two names and an address for you," the computer expert reported.

"Hold on that," said Bolan. "How's Konzaki?"

"No change," reported Kurtzman. "April has a

guard on the door. Two doctors and a nurse are with him right now. It's all we can do."

"Any contact with Able Team yet?"

"Negative. We still can't get through. My guess is they're the same. I've got my crew working without break."

"Tell them to work harder. The Central Foreign Bureau has a mole inside The Dragon's operation. The CFB boss put it together and The Dragon has been tipped off about what's going down."

"Farnsworth, the bastard."

"That mountain fortress is a trap for Able Team. If we don't contact them to abort their mission in time, they'll be massacred by the force The Dragon left behind."

"It seems," said Kurtzman thoughtfully, "as if an awful lot is going wrong for Stony Man all at once."

"What's the status of Phoenix Force?" asked Bolan, ignoring Kurtzman's comment.

"On their way home. Their ETA is midnight."

"Wade. Did you run a clearance check?"

"April did. Our security officer has a clean bill of health, Striker, clear back to Nam. You want the details?"

"Later. Now tell me those names and address."

"Ismet Kemal and Mustafa Izmir," said Kurtzman. "Armenians. Chief enforcers for a terrorist cell operating out of Turkey that calls itself the Justice Commandos of Armenian Genocide. The CIA spotted them disembarking from an Istanbul flight late last night. We got our intel from the usual source, but the Company has it classified top secret.

"They have Kemal and Izmir under surveillance right now. That's how we know the address. I figured it might be more than coincidence, these boys in town when everything starts going to hell for us, especially since Kemal and Izmir's specialty is commando night raids. They've been linked to several such actions in Europe."

The Bear rattled off a street address that Bolan committed to memory.

"It's a start," said Bolan. He saw the runway lights of National Airport coming toward them.

"Thanks, Bear. Get through to Able Team the instant the communications foul-up is corrected. Gotta go."

"Roger," Kurtzman replied, and the connection was broken.

Grimaldi set the Hughes chopper down after control-tower directions to the airport's private landing area. The pilot cut the chopper's engine as soon as they touched ground.

Bolan climbed from the bubble front and shed the suit jacket and tie he had worn to meet the president.

He shrugged into a more comfortable jacket that once again concealed the Beretta 93-R.

"A lone-wolf play, just like it used to be," repeated Grimaldi as he watched Bolan tog for night work. The pilot wore an enthused grin. "Here we go again, is that it?"

"That's it," acknowledged the Stony warrior.

Bolan grabbed the briefcase containing his .44 AutoMag and more death.

APRIL ROSE ENTERED THE ROOM just as Aaron Kurtzman broke his connection with Bolan. She sat beside him at the communications console and handed him a cup of freshly made coffee.

"That was Striker," Kurtzman told her. He sipped the coffee and growled his contentment. "I gave him Izmir and Kemal."

April ignored her cup.

"I hope they're not a false lead."

"They're the only lead we've got," Kurtzman grunted. "Unless you consider Lee Farnsworth."

He briefed her on Bolan's report that Farnsworth had fingered the men of Able Team for a waiting Dragon in the Hindu Kush on the other side of the world.

April still didn't touch her coffee.

"Interagency rivalry? I've heard stories of it in the past."

"I barely survived two interagency wars," said Kurtzman. "Damn spy business."

"The damn spy business," said April. "Maybe that's what's been bothering him."

"You noticed it too, eh?"

"Of course I did, Aaron."

"If we're right, this thing could blow up in our faces, just like the plastique that blew out our communications setup."

"Mack won't risk Stony Man," said April. "He's committed to the new war."

"He won't risk us," agreed Kurtzman, "but he could reconsider if this is really where he belongs."

"That is his decision to make."

"Of course it is. I just don't want to see the man do something that'll burn all the bridges behind him."

"Like taking on Lee Farnsworth?"

"Farnsworth and his organization. Interagency feuds are strictly verboten. Farnsworth should never have betrayed Able Team to The Dragon, but if Striker executes Farnsworth or any of his people over this, all of those bridges will be gone and Striker himself will be ordered terminated. It's a tough game and those are the rules."

"Maybe Farnsworth and his unit aren't involved," said April. "We don't have proof. Only the timing, and that could be coincidental."

"We do have Izmir and Kemal," added Kurtzman. "I'd give anything to have those creeps be the source of this trouble."

"It's happening so fast," noted April. "First, the sabotage, then Konzaki and Able Team and now Farnsworth. It could be that there isn't a thread connecting it together."

Kurtzman got up and walked over to a window. He stood looking out at the night. His right hand rested on the butt of the holstered pistol April had brought him.

"I'm just glad we're carrying our own side arms tonight," he growled. "It's going to be a night for everyone to cover his own ass. I can feel it out there. I just hope to God Striker is aware of what he's up against. Washington is a goddamn snake pit. The only things Bolan can trust tonight are the guns he's carrying."

"He knows," said April.

The door opened.

The nurse who had been attending Konzaki stepped in.

April knew right away.

"Konzaki. . . ."

The nurse shook her head.

"I'm sorry. There was nothing we could do. He never regained consciousness."

Kurtzman remained looking out the window. He did not turn.

"Why?" he said into the night.

BROGNOLA AND THE PRESIDENT were alone in the Oval Office. The Man himself had mixed the drinks, but the atmosphere was not congenial.

"I assure you, Hal," said the president, "I had no idea what Farnsworth was up to. I am purposely not briefed on the details of his operation, just like with Stony Man."

"I only hope Kurtzman restores our communications in time to alert Able Team to abort their hit on The Dragon," said Hal. "Those are good men, sir. We can't afford to lose them."

"I appreciate what you're saying," said the Man. "But I hope you'll pardon me for pointing out that you probably feel right now exactly what Farnsworth felt when a Stony Man operation caused the deaths of several of his men. Those were good men too."

Hal finished his drink, wishing more than ever for a cigar.

"A damn can of worms," he acknowledged. "And I've got a hunch it's all going down right now."

"Tonight?"

"Yes, sir. The colonel makes a damn good case for thinking there could be an attack on the Farm tonight."

"Farnsworth? You can't be serious."

"We don't know for certain who's behind it. Colonel Phoenix is working that angle. And our intel informed us that Armenians could be involved, with or without the CFB. Or there could be factors we don't even know about yet."

"Armenians?" said the president. "No, don't tell me. If my political opponents ever got hold of this kind of thing, I'd be roasted alive. What about Colonel Phoenix? The man concerns me."

"In what way, sir?"

"He's the only guy who ever told me to go to hell in this office," said the president with a chuckle, "but I don't mind that. In fact, I like him for it. I know of his work during the Vietnam War and his own Mafia campaigns, and I have a sketchy idea of what he's accomplished for Stony Man.

"His ideas of right and wrong have thus far happily coincided with our ideas of right and wrong."

"Bolan will not move against Farnsworth or the CFB unless he has positive proof," Hal assured the president. "The only indication we have of any possible involvement by Farnsworth in our trouble at Stony Man is the timing of it and his campaign tonight to put us out of business."

"But let us imagine the worst," suggested the president. "Suppose Colonel Phoenix does find out that Farnsworth and his unit are involved. I can't have him declaring war on Farnsworth and his unit and wiping them out. Colonel Phoenix has always gone by 'an eye for an eye,' and won't that be the way he'll see it if he does find proof of wrongdoing by Farnsworth?"

"I, uh, suppose it could be," hedged Hal. "But one thing you can count on with Mack Bolan is the totally unexpected."

"That's what I'm afraid of," the Man replied. "We're expecting the colonel to be a team man tonight. But when he stomped out of here a while ago, he did not look like someone about to play by the rules."

"The guy's a survivor," said Hal. "Rules only work sometimes."

"He'd better be a survivor if he breaks my rules," growled the president. "I do not want the man liquidating other American agents, no matter what the circumstances."

"That's putting the guy in one hell of a squeeze, isn't it, sir?"

"He's not the only one. I like and admire the guy, but I won't have any choice, Hal, if push comes to shove. Colonel Phoenix will be liquidated before he can make waves that will endanger our national security and this administration. I suggest you make contact with him to apprise him of this fact."

"He well knows the chances he's taking, sir,"

said Hal. "The personal consequences of his actions have *never* stopped Mack Bolan from doing what he had to do and they won't stop him tonight."

8

Bolan had already clashed with Armenian terrorist groups once before in his new war.

They wage an ongoing war of their own against the modern Turkish government for the twenty-year holocaust at the turn of the century during which millions of Armenians had been reportedly slaughtered by the Turks.

Denounced by all international Armenian communities, the terrorists had been gunning down diplomats and blowing up Turkish businesses and political concerns for decades. One week earlier a bomb had exploded at a Turkish airline counter at Orly Airport in Paris, killing six people and maiming a dozen other tourists. Only two of the victims were Turks. The Justice Commandos of Armenian Genocide had bragged of responsibility for the slaughter.

Lately, more and more of this terrorist activity had taken place on American soil.

Now came Kemal and Izmir.

THE ADDRESS WAS a secondhand furniture store on the fringe of the ghetto, not far from the White House.

The store was on a side street, the entrance three steps below sidewalk level, sandwiched in at midblock by a squat line of dark business fronts.

At the far end of the block, a single streetlamp cast a dull glow that extended only halfway down the street.

Bolan stood in deep shadow up the street from the store. He surveyed the neighborhood, attuning his combat senses to this probe.

The night was warm, the city sounds muted by the breeze that now carried the smell of rain with it.

The street was lined with parked vehicles.

Bolan spotted the pinpoint glow of a cigarette from a sedan parked at the opposite end of the block from the streetlamp.

Company men.

He backtracked away from the sedan, toward the dim streetlamp, and the man, or men, in the car did not see him. Or they did not care.

He rounded the corner building and moved past his parked rental car to the mouth of the alley running behind the shop.

The half moon was blanketed out by the low-hanging thunderheads, making the night blacker than usual in the confines of the alley.

The nightscorcher palmed the Beretta as he jogged down the alley to the rear of the address he wanted. He soundlessly negotiated a ten-foot wooden fence.

Bolan dropped to a crouch at the base of the fence and scanned the area behind the shop.

He saw the outline of a sentry against the lighted back window of the house.

Bolan came in at the man with a slashing chop that connected the butt of the Beretta with the base of the man's skull. The guy's knees buckled as he collapsed with a soft moan. Bolan caught him before he touched ground and dragged him off into deeper shadows away from the enclosed porch and back door of the shop. He left the sentry propped against the building.

The night warrior returned to the porch and the door, the top half of which was lighted window, unshaded.

Bolan moved in at a low crouch. He pressed himself against the door and risked a look inside from a corner of the window.

A conference between three men was in the process of breaking up at the far end of a corridor that ended at the front door of the house.

The men grouped around the door were swarthy, stocky.

Armenians.

Two of the men, wearing jackets, were checking their weapons.

Ismet Kemal and Mustafa Izmir toted short, compact Ingram Model 10 submachine guns, the "room brooms" of urban terrorist action.

The two men holstered their weapons in specially designed slings under their jackets, then grimly shook hands with the third man who held the door open for them and saw them into the night in a wordless parting.

The Armenian closed the door after the men and turned to walk back further into the house. Bolan figured that he could only be the Washington contact for the Istanbul hit team.

The man half turned toward Bolan when the Executioner sent a kick at the back door that broke the wood panel inward.

The surprised Armenian reacted with a curse as he grabbed for holstered hardware. But he was too slow. One whispered chug from the Beretta punched out the swarthy guy's left eye and made him dead meat. The corpse was still tumbling to the floor when Bolan withdrew to the backyard. Not pausing in his steady jog, he squeezed another 9mm slug from the Beretta as he moved past the unconscious sentry. He would never regain consciousness.

Bolan scaled the wood fence again without slowing and was on the move the instant he landed in the alley.

He trotted to the alley entrance and made it behind the wheel of his rental car. The Ford in which he had seen the pinpoint glow of a cigarette was just gaining the intersection up the block at a moderate, almost lazy speed.

The vehicle, driven by either Kemal or Izmir, would be somewhere ahead.

Bolan gunned his own vehicle to life and punched on the headlights as soon as the Ford was out of sight.

Bolan's rental Mustang pulled onto the street a half block behind the unmarked CIA car.

It was a parade through the night streets of Washington. Company men in the Ford were following the Armenians, and Bolan was tracking the CIA agents.

The three cars connected with Rhode Island Avenue and tracked northeast out of the lower-income neighborhoods through the stretch of commercial zoning that began to give way to more sleepy suburbs just over the Maryland line.

Bolan played the moderate evening traffic with all the finesse at his command, keeping the Agency car in sight but staying far enough away not to arouse suspicion.

They had just passed the Mount Rainier turnoff when Bolan realized that the group had picked up another member: a custom-designed van was doing its best to hold back from Bolan's Mustang. But the highly polished chrome work of the flashy vehicle stood out like a beacon as it drove under the street-lamps.

A new twist in an already tangled night.

In Brentwood, the group led off Rhode Island Avenue into a quiet neighborhood of winding streets lined and shadowed by white oaks, with one- and two-story residences interspersed with some office buildings.

Bolan knew where they were heading.

When he saw the Ford with the CIA men glide to a stop at the curb, not more than one block from where the Interstate Loan Association had its offices, he knew there had been too much coincidence this night.

Mack Bolan's former Mafia war had brought him

blitzing to this area when he targeted the Gus Riappi family and rained hellfire upon it.

At that time the Interstate Loan Association had been a money-laundry operation for the family that Bolan had somehow not had time to take out completely. Riappi still ran a weakened but functioning operation in the D.C. environs.

Mafia.

He would make time for dealing with this old enemy that appeared to be a link in the chain of events that occurred tonight.

He wheeled the Mustang off the track, cutting onto a side street that intersected the block where the CIA car had pulled over. When he was out of their range of vision, he coasted to the curb and killed the headlights and engine. He paused behind the steering wheel a moment more.

In his rearview mirror Bolan saw the customized van turn off the parade route and slide into deep shadows in the block behind him, facing in the opposite direction.

It occurred to Bolan that he had still not caught glimpse of the car carrying Izmir and Kemal since the trek began.

Now, the parade was over.

The players were in place.

The low ceiling of thunderheads rumbled ominously as if impatient for this action to begin.

Bolan strapped Big Thunder low on his right hip, unleathered his Beretta and went EVA into the night.

Into the killing ground.

WHEN THE TOYOTA he was tailing turned into a parking lot, CIA agent Bob Gridell steered his unmarked Ford Granada to the curb and doused the lights and engine.

The Toyota driven by Mustafa Izmir was out of sight somewhere on the blacktop on the far side of a low brick office building.

For a moment Gridell found himself wishing that he was across the river in suburban Arlington with his family.

Tonight was his second pull of duty after coming off a two-week vacation with Margie and the kids.

At forty-six, Gridell thought he was getting too old for this kind of work. Then he blocked those thoughts and checked the action of his pistol, a snub-nosed .38-caliber revolver.

He holstered the gun and reached for the under-dash mike of the car's two-way radio. He glanced sideways at his partner.

Robbins was also doing a last-minute check, his own piece a .45-caliber automatic.

"It's going down," Gridell told the younger man. "Our marks will hit that building on the corner, I'll lay you any odds."

"Bad odds," grunted Robbins. "You haven't been wrong yet. We'll have to take that building from both ends."

Robbins got out of the car. He closed the door soundlessly and stood scanning the terrain.

Gridell contacted their control and reported their position and what was going down.

"Do you require backup?" asked control.

"Not at this point," said Gridell. "Keep a unit standing by. This might not be the biggie. Don't want to spook these boys before we know what they're up to."

"We just hit the shop where they made their connection," said the control crisply. "We found two dead Armenians. One in the house, one out back."

"Damn. It couldn't have been our boys. The contact was alive and well and saw them out the door. We saw it."

"There is a wild card," acknowledged control. "A man named Phoenix. That's all we have at this point. It's top security, but we're breaking it a piece at a time."

"Keep me posted," said Gridell. "Right now, I've got two sightseeing Armenians to check up on."

"Be careful," said control.

"Always," said Gridell, and he broke the connection.

He joined Robbins outside the car.

Bob liked Dave Robbins. The younger guy had only been with the Company for eight months, all of that time spent assigned to apprentice under Gridell. The two had not yet seen action as a team.

Guns in hands, they split up wordlessly, moving toward opposite ends of the building at the quiet intersection.

As he jogged along, Agent Bob Gridell's spine chilled. He hoped he would not die tonight. I'm getting too old for this, he thought again.

Two terrorist hit men.

A rookie partner.

And now, a wild card named Phoenix.

TWO MEN HAD DINNER in the private room of an exclusive French restaurant on Q Street in Georgetown.

"Tell me about Phoenix."

"I followed your instructions. I put two men on the CIA stakeout of Izmir and Kemal."

"Can they be traced?"

"To us? Of course not. I'm not using our own personnel on this. Not with Phoenix."

"What are their orders?"

"Phoenix is screwing up a Company operation. He could get caught in a cross fire."

"With a little help."

"Yes, with a little help. My men have been told to hold back. If the CIA doesn't hit Phoenix and if those Armenians don't get him, then my people take him out. I don't care how good the bastard is. He's boxed in, and he doesn't even know it. He's dead."

"What about Stony Man Farm?"

"Our contact inside is in touch. They're still without satellite communications. One sour note. Phoenix has requested a double check on all Farm security clearances."

"Is that bad?"

"I don't think so. Our contact is being doubly cautious tonight, that's all. After tonight, it won't much matter."

"What time do you attack?"

"Don't you think it's best to keep you in the dark on some things, sir?"

"Yes, you're right. I'll need to appear suitably surprised. But it is tonight?"

"It's tonight. Tonight we level Stony Man Farm *and* Colonel John Phoenix."

9

A row of brick houses occupied the east side of the street, opposite the offices of the Interstate Loan Association. Light shone from some of the windows, but most of them were dark.

The Executioner moved through backyards, silently negotiating shrubbery and at one point a five-foot-high chain link fence. The moving shadow encountered no one in the night. Twice he spotted the bluish glow from television sets behind windows, but that was all. There was no nightlife in suburbia. Not from its inhabitants, at any rate.

Bolan advanced on the loan office via a circuitous route that brought him to the building from its northeast corner.

A Toyota was parked at the curb of the street where blacktop met a row of four-foot-high hedges that ran back from the street to disappear behind the darkened building. The hedges divided the Interstate property from its neighbors.

Bolan scanned the night with cold eyes and a colder Beretta as he came within ten feet of those hedges.

Suddenly he stopped.

He saw blurred movement near the inky splotches of shrubs adjacent to the parking lot.

Bolan could barely make out a figure, several yards down, gripping a rifle. Closer toward his own position, he could discern more clearly the figures of two men, standing together. These men were carrying Remington 870 pump shotguns.

They had Mafia written all over them.

They were lying in wait, obviously. Their attention was focused on the parking-lot entrance of the Interstate Loan office.

Bolan was putting two and two together in his mind and very quickly getting a read on what was going down here. But he had to be sure before the killing started.

There was no sign of the Armenian terrorists, Izmir and Kemal. They had already entered the building.

There was only one way Bolan could confirm what he was thinking.

He crouched slightly, ready to spring into the deeper shadows around him if he had to.

"Identify yourselves," he said quietly.

The whispered words cracked like a gunshot.

Shrubbery rustled as all three men spun around in the direction of Bolan's voice. The man up the line stayed where he was, melding with the shape of the hedge.

Three shotguns pointed at Bolan.

The men who had been waiting along the hedge were all cut from the same mold of beefy hulks in expensive street suits. But the shotguns did not look out of place in their hands.

The one nearest Bolan, hulkier than the others, spoke to the nightfighter.

"Identify your own damn self."

"Frankie. From New York," said Mack Bolan. "I've got a black ace of spades in my wallet, soldier. Come here and take a look."

There was hesitation from the men drawing beads on Bolan.

Ace of spades.

The anonymous calling card of the Mafia's autonomous enforcement arm. The Black Aces.

The aces were a traceless crew of killers who altered their looks with plastic surgery so often to match new names that even they themselves might not remember how they began. They were the gestapo of organized crime, responsible only to the ruling *commissióne* in New York. The elite unit kept undesirable hands out of the till and the rightful percentage of *commissióne*'s tax funneling through laundered setups like Interstate.

Mack Bolan, a master of role camouflage all the way back to Nam, had penetrated Mob defenses posing as a Black Ace before.

"You better tell me more," snarled the voice to Bolan, cautious but a little respectful.

"There's no time for bullshit, soldier," growled Bolan. He started advancing on the two men nearest him. "Check with Riappi if you've got a two-way."

Bolan paused within four feet of the two nearest men.

He held the Beretta down at his side. They stood with shotgun barrels still pointing at the center of his chest.

"Uh, maybe I'd better see that card," growled a

voice from behind one of the shotguns, and Bolan knew they'd bought it.

Bolan slowly brought out his wallet with his left hand. He did not break eye contact with those he knew would be gauging his every move from behind the Remingtons. He extracted the ace of spades and extended it.

The guy to Bolan's right reached out for it. Bolan could have killed the guy then, but the odds were against him. The other soldier standing next to the spokesman had his shotgun trained on Bolan. Still another hardman would be covering this confrontation some yards away.

The man who took the card studied it, made a grunt of assent and handed the card back to Bolan. He lowered his shotgun as he did so.

"Put it down, Chuck," he instructed the man next to him. "Can't be too careful," he said to Bolan. "You know how it is."

Then the guy made a waving motion to the hardman down the line and that gunman returned his attention to the Interstate building and the parking lot.

Bolan pocketed the specially laminated card that he always carried even though the Executioner's war against the Mafia was a thing of the past.

"I know how it is. You the headcock here?"

"Yes, sir. My name's Giancola. The boys call me Pepsi."

"Riappi didn't say anything about backup?" asked the Executioner.

"No, sir, no backup. Just me and Chuck and

Horse down there. Uh, sorry, sir, about drawing down on you like that.''

"You did right, Pepsi. You call me Frankie."

"Uh, sure, Frankie. Thanks."

"You going to call Riappi?"

"Naw. No one knows about them black cards, sir, uh, Frankie, except the organization. Impersonating one is suicide.''

Bolan nodded toward the dark Interstate office building beyond the hedge.

"The Armenians. You going to hit them when they come out?"

The headcock nodded.

"They figure to find Mr. Spinelli and his men in there in the basement cutting up the day's take like always. The guy who set us up for them is on our payroll. When these crumbs don't find nothing, they pull out. That's when we mow their asses down. But, uh, of course, now with a Black Ace sent down to handle this, uh, if you got any other ideas, Frankie?"

"I've got an idea," acknowledged Black Ace Bolan.

He raised his Beretta and blew away a chunk of Pepsi Giancola's skull.

The mob headcock was still pitching backward into the hedge when Chuck brought up his Remington pump shotgun. But he was not fast enough to stop Bolan's Beretta from tracking sideways like lightning and spitting another 9mm challenger that blasted a hole through Chuck's left nostril.

Horse, several yards away, heard the silenced

chugs of the Beretta. He called out in a hoarse whisper.

"Hey, what the hell? Pepsi?"

Bolan fell away in a racing half-circle to come up behind the third mobster.

The Executioner materialized out of the shadows behind Horse. His left arm went under the hardguy's throat and yanked him back.

Horse dropped his shotgun.

Bolan smashed the butt of his Beretta down against Horse's skull hard enough to cave in the man's head.

Bolan released the dead body and cautiously advanced toward the building. He came to a side window facing away from the parking lot.

He tapped the corner pane of the window.

The glass fell inward. Bolan reached in and unlatched the window. He raised it and climbed in, lowering it behind him. He crouched in the darkness of a room, waiting to see what the noise of the shattering glass would bring.

As his eyes adjusted to the gloom, he realized he was in some kind of an office. He made out the forms of a desk and filing cabinets.

The noise brought a response from outside. Bolan heard approaching footsteps and a whispered exchange.

"Here's a broken window," a voice said close to where Bolan crouched with the Beretta, ready.

"And here's a damn sight more," an older voice said from a bit farther away. "Jesus for breakfast. Three dead guys. I wonder. Phoenix."

"You call it, Bob," the younger voice said.

"We go back out front," said the older man. "Be careful, Davey. Three dead already. Whatever way this breaks, there's going to be more blood."

"You too," said Robbins, and the footsteps padding out of Bolan's earshot.

It played clear enough to Bolan. The Mafia thought they were canceling out two Armenian strongarms most likely seeking revenge in a drug deal turned sour. The Riappi family had conned the terrorists who supported their activities with drug trafficking. The Justice Commandos of Armenian Genocide were out for blood and were supposed to walk to their deaths when they thought they were hitting a family bank.

Bolan moved out of the office, into the main corridor of the unlighted Interstate Loan Association building.

He heard whispered voices, foreign, guttural, from the end of the hallway.

Bolan flattened himself against the wall, bringing up the Beretta and flicking the 93-R to its automatic three-shot mode.

He had found Ismet Kemal and Mustafa Izmir, the terror merchants from Istanbul.

The Armenians sounded angry after finding an empty building where they had hoped to recoup their losses.

The Executioner raised the Beretta to terminate these scum.

A door latch clicked.

Kemal and Izmir ran from the building, not even

aware that quiet death was so close behind them.

Bolan went after them.

BOB GRIDELL CROUCHED near some rhododendron bushes that he hoped offered him some cover. He had a clear view of the glass door that led to the parking lot where the Toyota sat. The CIA man held his .38 revolver in standard two-handed grip.

Gridell's rookie partner, Robbins, was in a similar stance behind some shrubbery on the other side of the door.

Gridell hoped the kid would do all right tonight.

The door swung outward without noise.

Agent Gridell saw it and tensed.

Two men rushed out of the building, walking briskly toward the car: Izmir and Kemal.

"Freeze right there," Gridell snapped from cover of darkness. "You two men. Raise your hands."

The Armenians moved away from each other to opposite sides of the Toyota.

The terrorists raised their submachine guns and opened fire. The angry chatter of automatic weapons split the night and illuminated the killzone with wild strobelike flashes.

Gridell felt an excruciating blaze of pain as he slammed into the ground. He knew that he was hit in his right leg.

"Bob!" cried the younger agent's voice with the shock of seeing Gridell go down.

Robbins materialized from the gloom off to the right, advancing cautiously but still anxious to reach his partner. The two terrorists saw him. The Armenians swung their machine guns in Robbins's direction.

From where he lay on the ground, Gridell felt the hot flashes brought on by loss of blood. He swung his .38 around to track on the two hit men.

"Dave! Fall back!" Gridell shouted weakly.

The Ingrams opened up again.

A tight pattern of double-figure-eight automatic fire hammered Robbins. He twitched and jerked in a wild shudder of rupturing flesh and spraying blood.

"Dave!" screamed Bob Gridell even as he triggered off two fast rounds that thwacked into Ismet Kemal and blew away his face.

Then the wounded Company agent saw the second terrorist tracking his machine gun toward him. In that instant, the CIA man *knew* he was too old for this work when he saw Death aiming at him.

Then a totally stunned look appeared on Izmir's face as a mighty unseen force made the terrorist stop in his tracks, then stumble a few feet and drop.

The back of Izmir's head was a bloody pulp.

A black figure, which for one crazed moment Bob Gridell thought was Death himself, emerged from the loan-office building.

Gridell saw a big man gliding over the killground, moving across the parking lot like a suburbanite out for a late-night jog.

Phoenix.

"Phoenix! Wait!"

The wounded agent forced himself to stand. Pain ripped through him as he came up on one knee.

He kept a tight grip on his .38.

Four rounds left.

The shadowy specter did not stop.

The night swallowed the wraith that saved Bob Gridell's life.

Grimacing in agony, Gridell hobbled after the nightscorcher.

He averted his eyes from the butchered remains of Dave Robbins.

BOLAN TRAVELED SOUNDLESSLY through the desolate backyards of suburbia.

The chatter of machine-gun fire in the neighborhood had naturally raised a furor.

The commotion brought frightened interest as night-robed suburbanites appeared on the front porches of the houses that faced the battle zone.

It was clear to the Executioner that he had followed the wrong trail, at least concerning the sabotage and probable imminent attack on Stony Man Farm.

The Armenian terrorists' arrival had been a coincidence.

There was nothing more for Bolan to do here.

Two Armenian enforcers were dead.

So were the Mafia killers who had come to ambush them.

Society would not miss them.

That was enough for Bolan.

A CIA agent died hard tonight. Another wounded, but not bad enough to keep the guy down.

Bolan sensed the wounded Company man on his trail even now, slow and painful, but sure.

This blitzer was withdrawing, rather than fire on an agent. And because this false trail had brought Bolan nothing but trouble, he needed answers.

Fast.

Who?

He was twenty meters from his parked Mustang, moving toward it fast when he saw the dark shape of the van across the intersection from his car. The van appeared not to have moved since following Bolan here.

The van.

The next step.

The nightfighter sensed rather than heard the rustle of movement from the darkness to his right and left.

The Executioner dived to the ground.

A twin barrage of automatic-weapons fire split the night from two directions, stitching the air around him with blistering fusillades of sudden death.

10

The ambushers were using flash suppressors.

Bolan could not tell from which direction the automatic fire issued, only that there were two gunners.

He hit the ground in a loose roll that took him out of their line of fire. Bolan did not return fire, but remained flat on the ground, knowing he would be an impossible target to find now.

There was a rustle of hurried movement somewhere in the night beyond Bolan's range of vision. He heard the slap of receding footfalls on the pavement.

The rental Mustang was now some forty feet away from Bolan's position.

From somewhere back in the vicinity of the Interstate Loan Association building, where the slaughter had just taken place, the wounded CIA agent would be closing in on him, Bolan was sure.

The sound of vehicle doors being pulled shut carried on the night breeze from the direction of the parked van.

Bolan started jogging toward the van.

As he silently glided past the Mustang, he reached down without slowing and picked up a fair sized rock from the garden of the corner residence.

In a crouch, the nightfighter angled closer toward the vehicle's occupants.

Bolan knew this play, a classic urban guerrilla hit tactic. *If* he was right.

When he was far enough away from the Mustang, he tossed the rock over his shoulder.

The stone hit the side of the rental car, and in the night air it sounded like the sedan's door being pulled shut.

Bolan charged at the van full speed now, the .44 AutoMag gripped in his right hand, but the vehicle was still another ten meters away from the intersection.

The Executioner braced himself as he ran.

He heard the explosion behind him an instant after the rock hit the Mustang. The blast lit up the night with a silver flash that rocked the ground under Bolan's feet.

He *was* right.

The Mustang was wired to explode in case the ambush was not successful.

The night blitzer looked back to see the rental car go up in a fireball eruption.

The van roared to life and the vehicle shot forward.

At first Bolan thought he would not catch the van before it got away.

But the driver decided to withdraw on the same street that led back to the main avenue by which the vehicle had followed Bolan there.

They were too sure of themselves.

The van swung in a screeching U-turn that almost capsized the vehicle.

The driver stood on the gas as the bulky vehicle lurched forward, accelerating the hell out of there—on a course that would take it right past Bolan's position on the tree-lined street.

Without slacking pace, Bolan reholstered the AutoMag. He used his momentum to jump and grab a low-hanging branch.

He hoisted himself up into the lower branches as the van gunned by beneath him. Bolan dropped onto the vehicle as it sped by, spraddling himself on the roof. He knew that the occupants of the hurtling van would hear the thump of his landing but not have time to react.

He gripped the left bar of the roof rack to steady himself on the slippery surface. With his right hand, Bolan pointed the .44 AutoMag into the cab of the speeding vehicle. He opened fire blindly.

Someone screamed shrilly.

"Agh! My ear! He shot off my fucking ear!"

The van reached the intersection.

The driver yanked to the left in a wide arc that caused the wheels to ride the curb with enough impact to loosen Bolan's grip on the roof rack, pitching him to the ground.

He landed on the springy turf of a well-tended lawn, coming out of the roll in time to see the glow of the red taillights diminishing in the distance as the speeding van rocketed past the hulk of the flaming Mustang.

The sound of squealing tires filled the night air as the fleeing vehicle began a mad swerving pattern.

The wandering van presented an almost impossible

target for the ace marksman. But Bolan decided not to risk a shot that could endanger innocent bystanders in this residential area.

He turned on his heel and jogged back along the street to where the CIA agents had parked their Ford near the Interstate offices.

Bolan saw no sign of the wounded CIA man who had started to follow him.

He reached through the driver's-side window of the Agency car and felt along the steering column. The keys were in it. He slapped the big AutoMag back into sideleather on his hip, then climbed into the Ford. The Executioner gunned the car to life and burned rubber in hot pursuit after the escaping van.

BOB GRIDELL'S HEART POUNDED against his rib cage like a jackhammer. The injured CIA man forced himself to walk along on the dark street in pursuit of the big gunman.

He paused for a moment when the chatter of automatic-weapons fire sounded from up ahead. Then he gripped the .38 even tighter in his right hand and pushed on, almost delirious with pain.

The shooting stopped as abruptly as it had begun.

Seconds later a loud explosion blasted the night, almost pitching him to the pavement.

Momentarily distracted by the eruption, Gridell sighted the unmarked Ford. Suddenly the vehicle roared to life and executed a squealing U-turn that left a smoking patch of rubber on the tarmac.

Gridell raised his .38 and assumed a shooting stance as best he could. Pain knifed through him as he triggered three shots after the receding car. The reports from his pistol thundered in his ears as he realized his shots were going wild.

The agent's own car was out of range.

The CIA man held his fire.

All he could do was helplessly watch the taillights of the Ford disappear into the distance.

The echo of gunfire faded from suburbia.

Residents got braver. They clustered along the tree-lined street that had so suddenly become a hellground. Curious chatter filled the air.

Gridell lowered his pistol.

He turned, wearily, painfully, forcing himself to limp back to the nearest house.

Six men dead, including a partner; a kid who never had the chance to prove himself.

A stolen unmarked car.

And a wild card.

John Phoenix.

11

Bolan caught up with the van on Rhode Island Avenue. It was heading southwest, back across the state line into D.C., retracing the route that had led the parade of death into Brentwood.

The Executioner held his tracking position as far back as possible.

Traffic along the main artery was even sparser than before, and Bolan realized the men in the van were not trying very hard to evade him, heavy traffic or light. Unless, of course, they were luring him into a trap.

John Phoenix intended to trail these rats back to their hole.

The Executioner would blow hell out of whatever rat hole the van led him to.

The trail was heading back to the sprawling ghetto.

He followed the van off the main avenues, away from the bright lights, to a city block of vacant tenements that loomed like monoliths against the cloudy night sky, a city block of condemned renewal.

Bolan watched the customized vehicle turn into a street flanked by deserted tenements and another block that had already met the demolition crew's iron ball.

It was a desolate scene in the middle of the city. The sounds of midnight D.C. were muffled, distant; it could have been a universe away.

The driver doused his headlights as the van came to a stop in front of an apartment building. Car doors opened. Bolan guided his own vehicle into a turn, out of sight, before the occupants of the van could turn fully around on their way into the nearest tenement.

They disappeared inside.

Bolan unleathered the AutoMag and padded after the two men.

He paused, flattening himself against a wall at the open entranceway to the condemned building. He held up the stainless-steel .44, ready for anything. Ready to kill. He eased into the tomblike shell that had once housed life but now only reeked of dry rot and decay.

He heard faint voices coming from down a dark corridor. The voices were muffled by walls.

Bolan kept his back pressed to the grimy wall of the corridor. He moved slowly, being careful to step only where the floor met the baseboard of the wall, avoiding any loose floorboards that could cause a warning squeak in a building this old.

He followed the sound of the conversation to a room where the door had been taken off the hinges. A rectangle of dull grayish light fell upon the scuffed floor of the corridor.

Bolan made it to that entrance in a half dozen soundless strides.

He stood just out of view of whoever was talking inside.

He listened.

"The bastard shot my fucking ear clean off!" a voice whined in agony.

Another male voice said, "You bleedin' like a stuck pig, Jimmy Lee."

"You made your report. Have him patched up, Sam," said a third voice.

"Uh, what about you and, uh, the lady here?" the second person asked.

"John Phoenix is dead, ain't he?" growled Boss Voice. "I plan to stay right here and keep on doing what I've been doing. Ain't nothing to worry about."

Bolan had heard enough. He stepped into the room.

Three black guys.

The driver, and a guy who held his ear and looked like all his blood was draining out of the wound where Bolan had shot him.

They were talking to a lithe black dude who wore a pair of slacks and nothing else. This guy was pacing back and forth between Sam and wounded Jimmy Lee. On a bed in the corner of the room lay a nude blonde.

She was at the precious stage between girl and woman, innocence and sensuality in equal measures.

Bolan guessed her age to be eighteen. Shoulder-length golden hair framed a pretty face with a smattering of freckles. Her blue eyes held a glazed look and perspiration glistened on her nubile body.

Bolan straddled the doorway, tracking the .44 to cover the three men.

He addressed the young woman without looking at her.

"You're in a killing zone, young lady. Back off."

"I'm Ali's woman. Go to hell, mister," she said rebelliously.

"Cap him!" hissed the half-naked dude.

All three men fell away in separate directions, clawing for hardware. Even the bleeding Jimmy Lee.

Bolan put the wounded man out of his misery with a .44 headbuster from Big Thunder that sprayed the wall behind him full of brains and skull bits.

Sam, the driver of the van, was tracking on Bolan with an Uzi that he had slung beneath his jacket; the gun he'd ambushed Bolan with. But Sam was too slow.

Big Thunder spoke again as another projectile opened Sam's throat. A gaping hole appeared in his neck. The guy shuddered and collapsed lifeless on top of Jimmy Lee.

Bolan heard the blonde shriek.

He whirled in a crouch, just in time to see Ali half dragging the naked blonde out of the doorway.

The young woman was stumbling along willingly after the black, as they disappeared into the corridor outside the room.

Bolan angled for a bead on the woman's boyfriend, but she kept getting into the line of fire.

Bolan realized that they were heading toward the front of the tenement building.

Bolan quick-stepped into the corridor just as the black guy and the nude blonde reached the front entrance of the building.

Ali still had a tight grip around the woman's wrist.

"Hold it right there, you two," ordered Bolan.

He sighted down the hallway on the man.

The blonde was still in the line of fire.

The man spun around, releasing the girl's wrist. He flashed his right forearm up under her throat, pulling her back against him as a shield. Ali raised the .45 and pressed the automatic's muzzle against the girl's right temple.

Her eyes flared with new panic.

Ali's arm crushed the breath out of her.

"Wait!" she screamed. "No!"

The black glared over her shoulder at the man with the AutoMag.

"Drop your piece, motherfucker, or I'll waste this bitch."

It registered fully with the blonde.

"Ali! What are you doing?"

Bolan had aimed at a spot between Ali's eyes, but there was death reflex to consider. The damn .45 could still go off.

The girl jerked her head sideways, away from her lover's pistol.

Bolan triggered a round and the minihowitzer recoiled in his hand, spitting flame and a .44 flesh-eater that blew Ali's .45 automatic to bits. The impact obliterated three of his fingers along with it in a violent red spray.

Ali snarled in pain like a wounded tiger. He released the blonde and shoved her at Bolan, delivering a brutal chop to the side of her neck with his good hand.

The girl's eyes rolled back in her head.

She was deadweight coming at Bolan.

Ali expected Bolan to catch the nude form.

Bolan sidestepped, the AutoMag tracking back to Ali.

In the heartbeat it took for Bolan to sidestep the blonde and let her collapse against the nearest wall, the wounded black dodged out of the condemned tenement, back onto the sidewalk.

Bolan raced after him.

The big blitzer cast a glance at the crumpled figure of a naked woman on whom the tables had turned. She was unconscious.

A car engine roared to life in front of the building.

The Ford that belonged to the CIA was stolen again.

Bolan reached the front steps of the deserted tenement just in time to see the Ford flash past a sporty Lancia that was parked near the tenement. The fleeing car disappeared from sight around the corner of the building.

Nothing moved.

Bolan held in a bitter curse that burned in his throat.

He turned and reentered the building.

He walked by the unconscious blonde into the room where he had killed the two other blacks.

Bolan checked the dead men's wallets.

Drivers' licenses identified the deceased as Sam Datcher and James Lee Brown. Some pictures, miscellaneous junk, what looked like a gram of coke wrapped in tin foil snug in each wallet.

And each pocketbook yielded two hundred fifty dollars in brand-new bills.

Bolan grabbed a blanket from the bed and went back to the young woman.

There was no time to waste. Gunfire in this area could go unreported. It often did. But Washington was the most policed city in the nation. The call-in could already have been made.

He wrapped the blonde in the blanket.

There was nothing erotic about her nakedness. She was too unconscious to be sexy.

He picked up the strap purse she had instinctively grabbed in flight. He checked the handbag and discovered the ownership papers of the Lancia.

He carried her outside.

He moved around the building where he had seen the sports car. He placed the girl in the passenger seat, then got behind the wheel. He went through her purse again and found the keys to the car.

He found something else in the young lady's purse that he checked on as soon as he steered the Lancia safely a couple of blocks away.

It was the lady's driver's license.

And the deadly maze took on one more curious twist.

The damndest one in a night of damnation.

Her name was Kelly Crawford.

Bolan felt his gut clench.

He checked Kelly's address.

General Crawford had a daughter named Kelly.

The same General Crawford who had been Bolan's commanding officer in Vietnam, and had been instrumental in setting up the Stony Man Farm operation.

Kelly Crawford.

The general's daughter.

Out cold in a blanket and nothing else in a car driven by Bolan.

Some night, yeah.

And the killing had only begun.

12

Bolan had not intended this night in Washington to be one of rescuing damsels in distress or engaging everyone he encountered in pointless firefights. Sometimes, though, a man is forced into pure reflex response.

Kelly Crawford, case in point.

Bolan braked the Lancia for a moment at a drive-up pay phone and looked up General Crawford's residence in an area directory. It was listed and matched the address on the license in the young woman's purse.

He drove west on Constitution, through the moderate night traffic. Cruising at the legal speed limit, he took the Roosevelt Bridge across the dark expanse of the Potomac into Virginia.

The blonde in the blanket and nothing else batted her eyes open as Bolan swung south in the direction of the general's home in the upper-class suburbs of Alexandria.

Kelly Crawford said nothing to Mack Bolan. She glared straight ahead into the night as he drove, pulling the blanket tighter around herself, not even acknowledging the man beside her with a glance.

Bolan could see nothing of General Crawford in

the girl's physical appearance. She must have taken after her mother.

Retired Brigadier General James Crawford and his daughter lived in a neighborhood of winding streets, the homes set back from the streets on manicured lots separated from each other by trees and evergreen hedge.

A porch light went on when Bolan wheeled the Lancia to a stop on the half-circle gravel driveway in front of a sprawling bungalow.

The door opened and General Crawford stood there.

The girl in the blanket ran past her father into the house, out of sight.

Bolan stepped in and punched off the porch light. He closed the front door.

The general watched the big man with steady eyes, noting the AutoMag holstered at Bolan's hip.

"Colonel Phoenix, would you mind telling me what the hell is going on here?"

The general's warm Arkansas drawl was taut with concern.

This man was the closest thing Bolan had ever had to a father figure, after his real father.

Sam and Elsa Bolan had instilled in their son the basic morality of right and wrong that inspired Bolan to this day.

General Crawford had taken a green young recruit and made of him a combat-hardened veteran. The general made a soldier out of Mack Bolan in Vietnam.

Crawford visited Bolan in the earliest stage of the

Phoenix program when Bolan had been holed up recovering from the plastic surgery that had transformed The Executioner into John Phoenix. There had been some briefings after that, but Bolan had not seen General Crawford from then until this moment.

Bolan nodded in the direction the general's daughter had taken.

"You've got some trouble, General."

"I've had trouble with Kelly since the day Lucy died eleven years ago. Come in, Colonel. Drink?"

"I could stand some coffee."

"In the kitchen."

Crawford led the way.

They sat at the kitchen table, waiting for the coffee to perk.

"I've only got time for a quick stop," said Bolan.

"Tell me what happened."

"Kelly has rough friends."

"A black guy?"

"Three of them. Two of them are dead. Datcher and Brown, if it matters."

"It doesn't. One got away?"

Bolan nodded. "Wounded."

"That would be Jones. Were they...harming my daughter?"

Bolan told the general what happened.

The general registered no outward emotion as he listened. He stood and prepared the cups of coffee.

"Tell me about Jones," Bolan requested when he finished his report.

The general handed Bolan a cup of coffee.

"Grover Jones. He started calling himself **Damu Abdul Ali** a few months ago."

"How long has Kelly known him?"

"A few months. I expressly forbade Kelly to see him again. She decided it was because he was black."

Bolan knew the general better than that.

"What was the reason, sir?"

"I told Kelly what I found out," said Crawford. "Jones was a GI stationed in Germany until eighteen months ago when he was busted as the head of a full-scale drug operation he operated on the base where he was stationed. The murders of a German national and a Turk were involved, but it was never proved that Jones pulled the trigger. None of it was ever proved, as a matter of fact. But there was enough circumstantial evidence to get Jones bounced out of the service with a dishonorable."

"How did he meet Kelly?"

"Jones fought the proceeding right to the end. He was stationed in D.C. while his appeals went through. Kelly was working as a cashier at a PX snack bar."

"Jones may have changed his name, but he hasn't changed his style," said Bolan. "The men I took out were hired hands to do the dirty work while Damu Abdul stayed out of the rough stuff with Kelly."

"What rough stuff?" asked Crawford. "What did Kelly get mixed up in?"

"Have you been briefed on the Stony Man situation, sir?"

"I, uh, know of the difficulties you're having with Lee Farnsworth."

"That's not what I mean."

Bolan told the general about the sabotage of the Farm's communications system and the blood hunt that had taken John Phoenix to the Mafia, the Armenians, the CIA and Grover Jones and his pals.

He explained to the retired officer that he still did not have any answers as to who was behind the sabotage that so endangered Able Team and put a good man in a coma.

"The only way it plays is that Jones subcontracted a hit on me," finished Bolan. "Whoever wanted me hit knew about the CIA surveillance on those Armenians. They knew enough to figure that I would try for the Armenians on my own because their arrival in the city coincided with the sabotage."

"The someone you want seems to know a lot," said the general. "Do you think Kelly would know who hired Jones?"

"If Jones is big enough to subcontract a hit, he's smart enough to keep that kind of information to himself," said Bolan. "If he did have a name, it'd be just another middleman like himself."

"You must have some ideas."

"Some," acknowledged Bolan. "That's another reason I brought Kelly home to you, sir, instead of dropping her off somewhere. I could use your help."

"In what way, Colonel? I had a hand in designing the Stony Man and Central Foreign Bureau operations, but security requires that I keep my distance from both units."

"That's why you're the man, sir. I want a full run-down on Lee Farnsworth. Everything that didn't make his 201 file. There should be a lot. He's been in covert operations a long time."

"Farnsworth? You don't think he's behind the sabotage?"

"There's as good a case against the CFB as there was against those Armenians," growled Bolan. "The timing is right."

"Colonel, believe me, Farnsworth is as much a patriot as you are."

"Then you won't turn up anything. You had access to that information when you considered Farnsworth for the job, didn't you?"

"Let me get this straight," said Crawford. "You're suggesting that the head of the Central Foreign Bureau is a mole out to destroy the Stony Man operation?"

"I'm suggesting nothing," said Bolan. "I'm still looking. And I can't afford to slow down." He got to his feet. "You'll have to excuse me now, sir. I'll keep in touch."

The general stood and they left the kitchen.

"I'll do as you ask, certainly," said Crawford. "I've known you a long time, soldier. Long enough to trust your judgment. I just hope you're wrong this time. About Farnsworth and the CFB, I mean. I feel the same way about that outfit as I do about you and the bunch at Stony Man."

The two men faced each other at the front door.

"I'll try to pick up Jones's trail," said Bolan. "Any idea where the guy hangs out?"

A voice answered from the top of the stairs.

"He hangs out at a club called the Tattle Tail," Kelly Crawford told Bolan. "That's T-A-I-L." She gave him the address. He committed it to memory. "A joint," she added, not moving from the head of those stairs. "A rough place."

Kelly had cleaned up her act. A shower had buffed her blond beauty to a fine glow. Even her wet hair did not detract from her fresh good looks. She was clad in a floor-length robe that clung to her figure.

"I'll take my chances," growled Bolan. "Thanks, Kelly."

"I'm sorry," she said quietly, not making eye contact with Bolan or her father. "I've been an immature, stupid fool. I'm sorry."

"You're home now," said the general. "That's the important thing. Rest up. We'll talk about it in the morning."

"I'm home because of this man," said Kelly. She looked at Bolan for the first time. "Who are you, mister?"

"The name is Phoenix," Bolan told her. "Kelly, do you have any other ideas where Grover will hole up if the club doesn't pan out?"

"If Grover isn't at the Tattle Tail, someone there will know where to find him," she assured Bolan. "It's his turf. He used to take me there so all his pimp friends could see his fine white bitch."

"Please, Kelly—" began her father.

"I was a fool, and I've got to admit it aloud to both of you or it won't mean anything at all," said Kelly. "I was slumming with some real slime, wasn't I, Mr. Phoenix?"

"The slimiest," Bolan acknowledged. "And one of them is still out there. Grover will need a doctor, but he won't go to a hospital. He's holed up someplace right now where he thinks he's safe. That's the edge I need. He won't be moving. I will. And I've got to start moving right now. Good night, both of you. And thanks."

"Thank you," said Kelly to the Executioner. "I thought I loved a man who cared about me. But all he did was use me. I guess he was using me all along. Thank you for saving my life and making me see that." Then she looked at her father and her voice quavered. "I'm sorry, daddy. I really am."

Then she turned and padded off down the upstairs hallway.

Bolan and General Crawford stepped out onto the front porch.

"My thanks too, Mack. It's good to see you again." Crawford saw only the Lancia in the driveway. "Take the Lancia, you'll be needing some wheels. Good luck. God bless you."

The two warriors shook hands, then embraced warmly like the brothers they were.

Bolan climbed into the Lancia and roared away from there, angling back toward the Roosevelt Bridge and D.C.

He would get rid of the Lancia at the first car-rental agency he came to. Then he would phone the general to pick it up.

He was driving a car registered to General Crawford.

That would make it easy for someone to identify.

Someone in the know, the general had said.

Who?

Farnsworth?

Could General Crawford be involved?

Bolan felt a flash of angry guilt at that last thought.

He pulled up at a pay phone by a closed service station. He dialed a number that was routed from a scrambler station in D.C. through a computerized reroute via Miami, Flagstaff and Missoula, Montana, before buzzing the switchboard at Stony Man Farm's central control.

April answered.

"Stony Man."

"It's me, mother hen."

Bolan could feel the woman of his heart smiling at him over the line.

"Striker, it's good to hear from you. How's it going?"

"Swinging. I could fill a book. What's the situation there?"

"Some very bad news, some not so bad. Konzaki is dead. He never came out of the coma."

Bolan felt something cold run down his spine.

"Now it's personal," was all he said.

"Maybe you should be back here," said April. "It's past midnight. If there is going to be an assault on the Farm tonight, shouldn't you be here?"

"I'm twenty minutes away," said Bolan. "You're just lonesome."

April chuckled, and the intimate sound of it made the warrior wish for one instant that he and this woman were together and none of this was happening.

"I'm lonesome for you, Captain Hellfire. Men, we've got plenty of. Phoenix Force arrived an hour ago."

"What about the communications repair?"

"That's the not so very bad news," said April. "The Bear is out there now. The parts just arrived."

"Still no word from Able Team?"

"Still no word. I take it you have no intention of returning here until and if you're needed?"

"There's a hot time in the old town tonight," Bolan told her. "I've got some more cage-rattling to do. Konzaki's soul won't rest until it's done. Neither will mine."

"Hal has been calling. He wants you to contact him."

"I'll bet he does. Tell him the trail's too hot right now for talk."

"Is there anything I can do?"

"Run a tracer on Grover Jones, a.k.a. Damu Abdul Ali. Recent dishonorable discharge from the Army."

"Will do. Anything else?"

"Uh, yeah. See what you can come up with on General James Crawford."

"The general? But, Mack—"

"Someone close to us is striking at us tonight," Bolan explained. "My only course is not to trust anyone."

"You can trust my love, guy," April said softly. "I'll get what you need."

"Stay hard, lady," said Bolan.

He broke the connection.

The low cloud cover draped a humid blanket across Washington, as if trying to suffocate it.

Bolan returned to his vehicle and headed into the nighttime city, into the belly of the monster.

13

The Tattle Tail was in the heart of D.C.'s black section.

It had been a long time since the open racial hostilities of the late sixties and early seventies, but faces along the sidewalks and tenement steps turned hostile, cautious, at the sight of a white.

Bolan had shed Big Thunder, packing the minihowitzer away for the time being in its leather beneath the front seat of the rental car when he parked the vehicle half a block away.

He wore the Beretta 93-R shoulder-holstered beneath his jacket.

The inner-city pavement was crowded because of the warm spell, even though it was well past 1:00 A.M.

The street was alive.

Bright colors and the latest fashions paraded by to the throaty roar of powerful exhausts and the calls of young men to foxy ladies.

The tall man with peculiarly icy eyes ignored the stares and entered the bar that was advertised by a lone Pabst sign in the window.

The joint was busy with an after-hours crowd. The walls, hidden somewhere beyond a swirling haze of cigarette smoke, throbbed to pulsating funk music from a jukebox and the constant din of raised voices.

The conversation dropped when Bolan appeared.

Suddenly there was no sound except for the music.

Dozens of eyes watched the stranger from a sea of black faces.

Then the conversation and din of a barful of people resumed, a notch lower, but more guarded than before.

Bolan walked to the bar and took the end stool where the bar met the wall. There were no patrons back here except for the gaudy hooker two empty stools down.

The whore wobbled onto her high heels and started toward Bolan, but when she got close enough to read his eyes, she changed her mind and went back to her stool and her beer.

The bartender was a squat, round-faced man who came over and regarded the stranger with a careful appraisal that gave away nothing.

"What can I get you?"

The tall man issued a single icy command.

"Grover Jones."

"Uh, what's that, sir?"

The tall man with the icy eyes repeated, "Grover Jones. Calls himself Damu Abdul Ali."

The bartender's expression tightened into a strange mixture of apprehension and hope.

"You a cop?"

"I'm not his friend."

"Yeah, the punk hangs out here," the barman confided in a lowered voice. "I own this place.

Name's Ike. This joint used to be called Mr. Ike's, used to be a nice family place.''

Bolan looked around at the noisy hookers and pimps and ghetto nightlife.

''What happened?''

''Eight months ago this Ali bastard came around and said he likes my place and wants it as sort of his headquarters. Wants his own private rooms and his people to get cut-rate bar prices. I told him no, so he hired neighborhood gang kids to hassle my customers. They roughed me up. Said they'd do things to my wife and kid. My little girl, she's only fourteen. They changed the name of the place, everything.''

''I can do something about that,'' said Bolan.

The black proprietor regarded him for a moment.

''I'll damn well bet you can.''

''Where do I find Jones?''

''The rooms in back. There's a door to the alley, so I don't know if he's there or not, but some of his boys'll be. Be careful man. Them mothers kill people.''

''So do I,'' growled Bolan. ''Thanks, Ike.''

The Executioner left the bar. He skirted the bar scene and passed through the archway Ike had indicated. Off to his left were the restrooms. Another short corridor on his right led to a corner. He moved to the corner and around it. At the end of the hallway was an exit sign above a metal door with a push bar handle. There was another door to Bolan's left between him and the alley exit. The sounds from out front were a dull rumble back here. Bolan heard the soft, distinctive click of billiard balls from behind the door to his left.

He walked over and kicked open the door.

There were five people in the room, all black, all dressed in the latest fashions. Three guys were holding pool cues, one of them lining up his next shot on the green baize of the pool table. Two women sat at a private bar across the room, wearing the unmistakable attire of hookers.

Bolan came down three steps into what was decorated like a private club room. He walked over to the pool table. The two other men with cues stood at either end of the table. Bolan faced the guy who was about to make his shot.

"Ooh my, look what just walked in," said one of the whores.

Bolan addressed the guy across from him.

"I want Grover Jones."

The punk's shoulders hunched slightly. He did not look up. A cool one.

"Looks like we got a smartass honkey cop what wants his ass carved, boys."

The two men to either side of Bolan dropped their cues to the pool table.

Bolan allowed them to reach into back pockets and pull out six-inch blades that appeared with expert wrist snaps, learned only on the streets of the ghetto.

"That's how it is?" Bolan asked quietly.

The punk in front of him looked up and flashed Bolan a gold-toothed smile that was all hate and anger.

"That's how it is, motherfucker."

"Good," said Bolan.

Bolan felt himself going into an icy rage.

These were the cannibals who fed on their own—street bums who terrorized decent people too civilized and afraid to fight back. And Konzaki was dead.

Bolan picked up the pool cue set down by the punk to his right. He moved too fast for any of them to register a reaction short of startled grunts. He held the cue with two hands and lunged sideways so hard and fast the pointed end pierced the eye and brain of the guy on his right. Bolan yanked the stick out of the man's head and whipped it backward in a continuous motion with both hands. Bolan threw his weight behind the move hard enough to impact the second punk's forehead with death-dealing force. Both men collapsed on either side of the table, dead.

One of the whores screamed.

The guy across from Bolan lost his cool and his cue. He fished for concealed hardware, coming out with a .38 Saturday Night Special, tracking on Bolan real fast, fading back from the table.

Bolan feinted the guy like a fencer and flicked the stick.

The solid end of the cue clipped the pistol from the punk's hand before the guy could fall back far enough. Then Bolan cracked the thick end of the cue hard across the man's skull, knocking him to the floor.

The two hookers fled the room.

Bolan came around the table and grabbed the punk

by his shirtfront. He yanked the creep to his feet. He bent the guy backward across the elevated lip of the pool table.

The punk retained consciousness but almost lost it when Bolan rammed the man's head down onto the felt with a thump. The Stony chief leaned onto the cue that now held the black pinned across the throat.

"Where's Jones?"

Beads of sweat popped out like pearls on the punk's frightened face.

He cried out an address.

Bolan shifted his hold on the stick closer to the sides of the man's neck. He gave a mighty push on the cue, snapping the neck of the punk.

He stepped back and let the limp corpse sag to the floor to join the other two.

The Executioner's fury was abating.

They'll pay, Konzaki. Starting with these cannibals.

He tossed down the pool stick and walked out of the game room. He left the club via the alley exit.

No one tried to stop the tall man with the icy eyes as he disappeared into the night.

BOLAN DROVE PAST a one-story brownstone in a lower middle-class, racially mixed residential neighborhood. Dim light suggested itself from behind heavily draped windows.

It was the address given him by the black thug whose neck he had broken.

A man came out of the house. He strode briskly to the sidewalk and climbed into a parked car.

Two more men moved up the path that led to the front door of the house. They entered without knocking.

Bolan left his parked rental auto some distance down the block. He concealed the AutoMag under the driver's seat again. He preferred that whatever happened next not escalate into a firefight like the one back at the Interstate office.

The brownstone was the only house on the block showing any signs of life at this hour.

He walked up the front sidewalk, opened the door and stepped inside without knocking.

He was in a whorehouse.

He entered an old-fashioned parlor whose walls were lined with mirrors and couches, the couches occupied by whores of all shapes, colors and descriptions in various forms of intimate attire from lace to leather. The subtle strains of Muzak emanated from somewhere. There was a portable bar, and several men were in the first stages of appraising the merchandise.

Everyone casually looked around at Bolan's entrance.

Then not so casually as he strode through the room toward a hallway that led off the parlor to the private rooms.

"This is a raid," Bolan barked gruffly, throwing a thumb over his shoulder at the way he'd come in. "Everybody out."

There was a mad scramble as half-dressed ladies of the night and flustered johns poured out, looking for any available avenue of flight.

Bolan stalked into the hallway. He confronted two heavyset white men who appeared to be in charge, drawn by the commotion in the parlor.

Bouncers.

Digging for pistols.

With the edge of his flattened palm, Bolan hammered one guy at the base of the neck. The man slipped into unconsciousness.

The second man pulled out his gun.

Bolan executed a flying judo kick.

The pistol flew from the man's grip. He started to turn.

Bolan stepped after the guy, grabbing the bouncer by the collar. The Stony warrior flung him back into the wall with such force that the man's knees buckled and he collapsed.

Bolan knelt and grabbed the chucker's longish hair.

"Grover Jones. Where is he?"

The guy's eyes were glazed orbs. He pointed toward the back of the house.

"Number twelve."

"Thanks."

Bolan popped the back of the guy's head against the wall hard enough to knock him out.

He unholstered the Beretta and followed the instructions to the only door that was latched shut, around a bend in the hallway. All of the other doorways to the crib rooms yawned open from the haste in which the house had been vacated after the raid warning raised by Bolan.

Bolan stood back and to the side from the closed

door. He raised a foot and propelled two hundred-odd pounds of kick force, slamming the door inward off its frame.

The Executioner entered the dark room in a forward roll at the same instant that gunfire spit at him from a corner of the room.

Bolan came to his feet, tracking up with the Beretta, when the gunman made the mistake of trying for a better position. He moved across an unshaded window with enough streetlight outside to silhouette the ambusher.

Bolan tripped the guy, then slashed down with a well-aimed chop at the falling figure. There was a grunt of pain. A gun clattered to the floor.

Bolan took a second to step back and flick on the light switch. A bulb blazed overhead, revealing Grover Jones half sitting on the floor where Bolan dropped him.

Damu Abdul Ali glared up at the man with the Beretta. His right hand sported a heavy bandage where Bolan had shot off some of his fingers a few hours before.

"Who the—"

Bolan stood over him.

"That's what I want to know, Grover."

"The name's Damu Abdul, you mother."

The guy was trying to protect his bandaged hand by slipping it under his right thigh. Bolan grabbed Ali's forearm and stepped on the bandage, grinding it hard against the floor.

Jones let out an unearthly scream and thrashed onto his back.

"Your name is mud," said Bolan, aiming the Beretta at the man's black forehead. "That job tonight. You had Sam and Jimmy Lee follow those Company men until I showed up, then they hit me. Who told you where to sic them onto the CIA? That's Company business."

"I—I don't know," squealed Grover Jones. "Th-they'll kill me if I tell you!"

Bolan stepped down harder on the bandaged hand. Jones squealed louder, tears running down his face. Blood soaked the bandage.

"Okay, okay, please don't! The guy you want is Miller. Al Miller. He's got a place in Potomac!"

"More."

"That's all I know, I swear."

Bolan lifted his foot threateningly

"He. . .he's got some kinda troops out there. . .the guy's a merc. . .I knew him in the service. . .he fed me the shit on you and set it up."

Bolan stepped back, releasing the bloody hand.

Jones stared up at the snout of the Beretta that did not waver its bead between his eyes. The pain was suddenly forgotten.

"Wh-what now?" he asked.

"The payback," said the Executioner.

He blew Grover Jones's brains out all over the room.

The score is evening up, Andrzej.

Al Miller.

He stalked out of the house.

Back into the night.

Closing in.

14

Bolan cruised west on MacArthur Boulevard, then left the business artery to head for the grassy, hilly outer reaches of Maryland. He was looking for the county road listed under Al Miller's name in the Potomac telephone directory.

A stop at a twenty-four-hour convenience store gave him the directions he needed to find the Miller place.

The drive to locate the place consumed a half hour; thirty minutes Bolan knew he could not afford to waste.

It was not groundless paranoia that made Bolan think the world of Colonel John Phoenix was suddenly closing in on him, about to explode, taking everything with it.

Bolan realized that in the past twelve hours, his and John Phoenix's life had flashed past his eyes, not in some inner metaphysical sense but in actual flesh-and-blood reality.

Especially blood. During his search to find someone named Miller, the next link in tonight's blood-drenched chain, the Executioner had time to consider the strange, violent odyssey of this day and night.

In the beginning, it was like any of the other missions in this government-sanctioned new war against world terrorism: Mack Bolan, The Executioner, racing toward another confrontation with dark forces.

The Atlantic.

Terrorists.

The Dragon.

But this was only the beginning.

The stepping stone from then to now.

An odyssey to stun anyone's senses.

From an Oval Office briefing with the president to the cathouse depths of sewer city.

And between those two points?

The Mafia.

An old enemy, growing stronger again, probably overdue for attention from John Phoenix. If there would be a John Phoenix in the future.

Tonight, a lapse into automatic behavioral patterns from that past war against the Mafia: a Black Ace appeared from nowhere and right now the *commissióne* in New York would be madder than hell, shaking up everyone on the scene for an explanation of why a headcock named Pepsi Giancola got capped along with some street soldiers when it was Pepsi who was supposed to be snuffing out Armenian jerks.

It was almost like the old days when Bolan was alive. Yeah, exactly like an Executioner hit. But of course, Bolan is dead.

Armenians.

The CIA and the CFB and Lee Farnsworth and a murky world of clandestine espionage operations that Bolan never felt comfortable with.

Farnsworth was right, in a way.

Bolan was a soldier.

A combat specialist.

His place was on the front lines, like he'd told the president.

Striking at the enemies of the Phoenix war.

Tonight, the war came home.

At this moment, top priority continued to be *who*?

Who was Bolan's real enemy this night?

Somewhere in or around this city of lies, double dealing and treachery, a killer sat smug, thinking he was safe, that his trail was covered, that he could go on with whatever else he had planned for the Stony Man operation, tonight and anytime in the future. Someone who knew all the workings of the U.S. intelligence system from top to bottom.

This someone was Konzaki's killer and the true saboteur of Stony Man Farm as sure as Grover Jones and Miller and whatever other hired hands, hired death, were doing his bidding.

This was the one Bolan wanted more than any of these vermin. The one who pulled the strings and bartered in souls and sent people to their deaths when the whim moved him, hiding it all behind a cloak of influence.

This someone was evil moving among the good, indistinguishable, making him that much more dangerous.

But The Executioner was in town.

And that made all the difference in the world.

15

Bolan found the county road he wanted and began an initial recon to set the terrain of this action firmly in his mind.

At first glance the property owned by Al Miller was not unlike any number of similar ones in the area.

This was horse-estate country.

Miller had to be doing all right for himself, whatever his scam was.

Or he had solid backing.

Bolan guessed the latter.

The millionaire set liked its privacy. Formidable brick walls about ten feet tall surrounded many of these estates. There were huge expanses of uninhabited acreage in between.

Miller's guise of respectability lasted no longer than a closer visual as Bolan's rental vehicle glided past. The Executioner hoped that those inside viewed it as just another car passing in the night.

The main entrance to the grounds was set midway in the face of the walled perimeter that bordered the paved road.

A brick guardhouse sat behind an iron gate.

Bolan saw two sentries; they wore side arms and

there was undoubtedly heavier artillery, out of sight but close at hand.

When he reached the far end of the property line, Bolan continued to drive another quarter mile until the looming walls of the estate were blocked from view by a mild dip in the undulating Maryland terrain.

Bolan parked his car well off the blacktop, concealed from casual glances by a cluster of stately oak trees.

He strapped on Big Thunder.

This would be a hard hit.

He jogged back toward the walled property of Al Miller. He stayed off the road, approaching the side wall that connected with the one fronting the county road.

He was not ideally togged or rigged for a night hit. His dark sweater and slacks helped him blend into the night but his black combat grease had been lost when Sam Datcher and Jimmy Lee Brown blew up his rented Mustang at the Interstate Loan shoot-out.

Bolan hoped the moon would not break through the heavy clouds overhead, but that did not seem likely.

The Beretta 93-R rode ready in its shoulder holster and the AutoMag was fast-draw ready. Heavy artillery, sure, but it would be no heavier than the arsenal on the other side of those walls. His other instruments of death, such as the stilettos, garrotes and high-explosive grenades, so important on an assault like this, had also been destroyed in tonight's car blast.

The hell with risks.

The Executioner was blitzing.

He negotiated the wall with ease, landing on the other side without a sound.

He palmed the silenced Beretta.

He hoped Big Thunder would not be needed at all or only as a last resort to blast his way out.

He remained in a crouch, the 93-R ready. He scanned the darkness, his icy gaze encompassing the deserted grounds of the estate.

He saw no one.

Several lights illuminated a massive main house about eighteen hundred meters across a rolling, gradual incline.

Bolan padded cautiously toward the main house. The nightfighter kept to the shadows of the evergreens trees that dotted the landscape.

The Executioner met no interference.

Miller's place was guarded tonight by only a skeleton crew for some special reason. Or the man had nothing to hide and the gate sentries were only for show to grant the guy his privacy.

Perhaps this was another false lead like those Armenians. But Bolan didn't think so.

The night warrior moved on a course roughly parallel to the long, curved gravel driveway. He reached the edge of a tree line that yielded to a clearing surrounding the main house and another building. He paused for further recon.

Grover Jones's instructions had brought Mack Bolan to an expansive Colonial-style mansion. A huge courtyard was dominated by a large fountain

now artistically illuminated by multicolored flood-
lights.

The other building was a more modern, strictly
functional one-story prefab job, twenty meters from
the main house.

Barracks, thought Bolan.

There was no sign of human activity.

The area was graveyard quiet.

Bolan remembered the armed guards at the gate.

And the lighted windows in the main house.

There was a roofed porch on the south side of the
house, across an expanse of sloping lawn from Bolan's position. The stretch of lawn was bathed in
faint glow from the floodlit fountain.

Bolan decided to chance it.

He left the tree line. He made it to the porch and
holstered the Beretta. He pulled himself up onto the
roof. Then he palmed the 93-R again and stretched
out a leg to gain balance closer to the nearest second-
floor lighted window.

The window was open against the warm night.
Wispy drapes offered no privacy this close up. But
there was nothing to see. An empty bedroom. A light
someone had forgotten to turn off.

Bolan heard the unmistakable mutter of male
voices. Then a female voice, coming from the next
window down, also lighted.

A foot-wide ledge ran around the white stone mansion between its two levels. Bolan got a firm footing
and edged himself toward the window from which he
heard the voices coming.

He chanced a peek inside.

Another open window. A good view through lace drapes into another bedroom.

This one was occupied.

Three men and a woman.

The woman was clothed, but not doing too well otherwise.

She was tied to a straight-back chair in the middle of the bedroom, bound hand and foot and body with rubberized clothesline.

Bolan recognized the woman.

Tonight was an unraveling tapestry of this warrior's life. That's what throbbed and tried to close in and race past him at the same time, unbidden, but there just the same. His back pages and his destiny colliding on a warm spring night in Washington, when Death walked and his name was Bolan.

Her name was Susan Landry, investigative reporter.

Bolan would always remember Landry from his assault on the Mafia's Cleveland Pipeline during the Executioner's war against the Mob.

Landry was a woman no man would ever forget. Especially as a lover, as Bolan had been before he blasted Susan's father out of existence for his unholy alliance with the cannibals Bolan fought.

A lifetime ago, to John Phoenix.

The three hard-eyed men in the bedroom stood around Susan. One wore a shoulder-holstered .357. The other two had shotguns that now rested upright against a wall of the bedroom while they took a closer look at the beauty tied to the chair.

Her shoulder-length raven hair was mussed, and

she wore a bruise on her right temple that had turned purple. But Susan was just as foxy as Bolan remembered from that long-ago Cleveland action.

Susan's eyes darted rebelliously between the two men in front of her. Then she tried to glance over her shoulder at the guy behind, but she was too damn tough inside to show these creeps any fear.

One of the men reached over and stroked her face, then his hand drifted lower as he squeezed her breast roughly. He laughed when she didn't cry out.

Bolan saw red.

The man sneered, "A tough baby. I like 'em tough."

"Miller will skin you bastards alive when he gets back and sees what you've done," she snarled in his face.

"Maybe Miller ain't coming back," grunted the other man who faced Susan. He reached over as he spoke and idly flicked her skirt up around her waist, revealing smooth, panty-hosed legs that became beauty-queen thighs and sheer panties. "And if Miller comes back, maybe we'll be gone."

The hood behind her guffawed and started unbuckling his trousers.

"After we have some fun with you, bitch."

"I give you nothing," hissed Susan Landry.

Planting her feet firmly, she leaned forward in the chair, lifting its two back legs off the floor. Then she plunged backward. The chair landed with bone snapping impact upon the feet of the jerk who'd been so anxious to take his pants off.

"Oh, shit," he howled as he stumbled back, hopping about the room on one foot.

The other two started to laugh at their friend's misfortune.

Bolan aimed through the wispy bedroom curtains. The laughter was suddenly cut off as the Beretta whispered once. A 9mm slug drilled through the laughing mouth of one would-be rapist, creating a cavity that no dentist could ever fill. The man had not even begun to fall when the 93-R spit fire again, and the two hardmen toppled to the floor.

Susan Landry's eyes opened wide at the tall, icy-eyed man who suddenly appeared in the room.

The third hood forgot about his bruised toes and his unbuckled pants. He drew his .357 Magnum and had time to trigger off a shot at the darting figure who broke from the open window. The explosion reverberated like a nuclear blast in the close confines of the bedroom. The projectile whistled wide past Bolan's right ear.

The Executioner triggered another round from the Beretta, and the third punk joined his deceased friends in the corner.

"Holy Mother!" exclaimed Susan Landry. From her awkward position tied to the chair, she could not escape the drifting stench of burned cordite that stung her nostrils. She looked around at the three dead men who an instant ago had been about to harm her.

The big man chuckled as he holstered the 93-R and bent to yank loose the knots of the clothesline that bound her. "The name is John Phoenix, Ms Landry."

She stood up when she was untied and briefly rubbed wrists chafed raw from trying to break free. She did not take her eyes off this stranger, studying him intently.

"How do you know who I am?"

"Call me a regular reader of your newspaper columns," Bolan replied truthfully. He snapped a fresh clip into the Beretta and held the pistol out to her "Can you handle one of these?"

She nodded and took the pistol in a practiced grip.

"Thank you, John Phoenix. I have a car downstairs. I drove into my own trap, you see. We can drive out of here."

She did not recognize Phoenix as Mack Bolan. There was no reason for her to. Plastic surgery had altered Bolan's appearance.

They hustled from the bedroom death chamber like a well-rehearsed team, Susan looking no worse for wear from her ordeal.

They hit an upstairs corridor and approached a wide staircase that led to a large foyer downstairs.

Susan and her rescuer were at the top of the stairs when they heard the clatter of footfalls somewhere below.

They saw two guys coming up at them along either side of the stairway. The two hardmen at the bottom grabbed for hardware then had time to do nothing but die.

Susan snapped off a coughing round from the Beretta that pitched one hood backward. If the slug did not kill him, then there was no mistaking the sickening crack as his skull hit the marble floor.

The Executioner triggered Big Thunder, sending hood number two into oblivion. A headless body flew backward as if tugged by an invisible string. Blood splattered the wall as high as the ceiling, then the body crumpled into a heap near the closed front door.

They left the house through a corridor that led to a side exit.

Bolan allowed Susan to lead the way.

They emerged into the night and into a parking lot on the blind side of the house from the floodlit fountain out front.

A half-dozen vehicles occupied the area, including a Datsun station wagon.

Susan led him to it.

"Any idea how many men we're up against?" Bolan asked.

Susan yanked open the door on the driver's side and slid behind the wheel. She reached for keys that were in the ignition as Bolan jumped in alongside her.

"Miller took the main force with him."

The car roared to life.

"Miller took them where?"

They sped along the driveway, hugging the tight curves. They raced past the fountain lights that illuminated the front courtyard.

"I don't know where they went," Landry told him. She wheeled into the straightaway toward the iron gates. "But I overheard him giving orders. There are two men at the gate. Hang on."

"You do the same," grunted Bolan. "Good luck, lady."

Landry aimed the vehicle on a direct course for the iron-grille gate, where the two guards stood with shotguns, alerted by the sound of the revving engine.

The stunning brunette twirled the steering wheel hard to the left. The tail end of the wagon skidded to the right, gouging the trimmed edge of the turf. The Datsun stopped its slide, the passenger side parallel to the guards' left flank.

The sentries spun in Bolan's direction. Too late.

Bolan's AutoMag spoke.

The sentries were kicked backward from the impact of the .44 headbusters.

Susan left the car. These fresh kills were still shuddering in their own blood as Susan dashed to the guardhouse and activated the mechanical gate release.

She dashed back into the Datsun wagon and trod the gas so hard that the rear end of the subcompact danced from side to side as it sped through the gate.

The investigative journalist sped into the Maryland night.

Leaving Mack Bolan to wonder.

A fireball from his past named Susan Landry had reappeared.

It was all coming down.

Tonight.

A night of blood.

16

The vehicle driven by Susan Landry flew along the dark county road away from the Miller place.

Bolan holstered his AutoMag in its fast-draw rig on his hip. He reclaimed and holstered his Beretta.

"My car is in that clump of trees," he told her as they approached the spot where he had concealed the vehicle. "I suggest you come with me. This car is your death warrant if these people have the connections I think they do."

Susan cut her speed and guided the Datsun over the gravel shoulder and among the trees that Bolan had indicated.

"Miller has connections," she acknowledged. "You're right, of course. Care to give a lady a lift?"

Bolan's rented wheels were right where he left them.

"Wouldn't have it any other way," Bolan assured her, already climbing from the station wagon.

Landry briskly kept pace with him, easing into the passenger seat as he kicked the engine over, backed out and continued their course toward MacArthur Boulevard and D.C.

He felt her eyes appraising him in the darkness as he drove.

"Thank you for saving my life," she said.

Those were the exact words Kelly Crawford had used less than two hours ago.

What a night.

Without looking up, he reached for the pack of cigarettes wedged behind the sun visor above his head, stuck one in his mouth and lit it with the dash lighter.

Susan Landry had gone through changes since he last encountered her in Cleveland several years ago. Then, she had been an idealistic young woman; an idealistic young journalist. The toughness had been there, but not the maturity, the inner strength that had come from years as a roving investigative reporter.

There were character lines around her eyes that made her more beautiful than she had ever been before she had earned them.

"You got us out of there in one piece," he reminded her as he caught MacArthur Boulevard heading back into the city. The street was virtually untraveled at this hour. "You're a hell of a wheelperson, Landry."

He offered her a cigarette. She shook her head.

"I'm also a reporter," she said. "Even if I wasn't, I'd sure like to know what a man named Phoenix is doing stalking the wilds of Maryland like some jungle panther. Don't laugh. That's what you are, and mister, you look like pure trouble."

"Trust your instincts on this one, Susan. You're right. I am trouble."

"I'd say I was in a good deal more trouble before you showed up. I guess I will have a cigarette."

Her hands shook when she took the smoke from the pack and tried to light it.

"Let's trade," said Bolan.

"Fair enough. Ladies first, I assume."

Bolan grinned at her. He liked her style.

"Talk to me, Susan," Bolan said.

"I'm investigating the soldier-for-hire community that thrives in this city. Men with professional military training, soldiers, ex-government service people."

"Mercs," growled Bolan. "A real mixed bag."

Landry nodded. "And I drew the rottenest one."

"How did you hook up with Miller?"

"I was a disgruntled woman with a prison record. Bitter. Unable to find work. I knew some of the places in Washington where contracts for services in the merc community are lined up. I made sure I was in the right place at the right time. It goes with the territory."

"Miller must be pulling in some heavy bread to have a place like that in Potomac."

"He's paid well, but that house isn't really his. No one in the community knows that, of course. Say, this is the way to the airport...."

Bolan fired another cigarette. It was close. What he'd been tearing this town apart all night to find out.

"The house in Potomac. Did you trace it?"

"As far as a paper corporation operating out of an Arlington PO box. It dead-ended there. Why are we going to the airport?"

"I have a friend waiting there with a helicopter.

What was Miller doing behind those walls with all that acreage?''

"He was training men for night commando work. Where are we going in a helicopter?''

"How many men does Miller have?''

"He bragged to me about that. About twenty for the raid, not counting those scumbags he left behind to watch his place tonight. They were going to rip him off while he was gone and...''

Her hand with the cigarette started shaking again. So did her voice.

Bolan knew she was thinking how close she came to being raped. "Easy,'' said the big man softly.

She snapped out of it. "And you didn't answer my question. I thought this was a trade. Where are we going in a helicopter?''

They crossed the Wilson Bridge and swung north onto Mount Vernon Highway parallel to the river. The lights of Washington National Airport came into view up ahead to the right.

"*We* are not going anywhere in a helicopter. Do you have any idea what kind of target Miller was training his men to hit?''

"Not going anywhere,'' she echoed. "Then I guess our little trade is off.''

"Miller is taking orders from someone high up in the U.S. intelligence community,'' he told her.

He could feel her eyes spark with interest even in the dim interior of the car.

"Now we're trading. And I don't suppose you'll tell me who this person is?''

Bolan steered them into one of the airport approach lanes. He followed the curve away from the main terminal to the private landing area. He could see Jack Grimaldi's Hughes chopper waiting.

"I don't know who's giving Miller his orders," said Bolan.

Suspicions. They were all he had to go on right now and he could hardly breach the security of Lee Farnsworth, the CFB or General Crawford by dropping names to a journalist.

He braked the car to a stop near the chopper.

When Grimaldi saw who the driver was, he revved up the Hughes's engine. The rotors started whirling. The flight lights started blinking.

"I've only been...with Miller for two weeks," Landry told him, raising her voice to be heard above the throbbing rotor. "I've concentrated on the workings of his operation, the training of his men. I... assumed they were training for action in some other country. I never realized—"

Bolan had no more time. He opened his door and gave her a last look.

"Take the car, Susan. Go somewhere and find yourself a typewriter and write whatever you want about Miller."

"What about you?"

"If you write about me, some good people will have their cover blown and probably die."

"So it's like that?"

"That would be a hell of a way to repay me for saving your life, wouldn't it?"

She laughed. A nice sound.

"You bastard. You're used to having your own way, aren't you?"

He started out of the car.

"Take care, Susan. Good luck."

"Wait a minute, soldier. You are talking to the world's most hardheaded woman. I don't get off this easy."

He paused, not mistaking the determination in those sharp blues. He saw the same look in the mirror whenever he shaved.

"Susan, I can't take you with me. I know where Miller is planning his hit. You told me enough for me to know it's going down tonight. Or this morning. I've got to do what I can to stop it from happening."

"You are not going to stop me from going with you," said Landry, distinctly enunciating each word.

"Sorry, lady, but I've got to," said Bolan sincerely, and he formed a loose fist and popped her one on the jaw that pitched Landry's head against the seat. He felt the pulse and nodded, satisfied she was unconscious, but unhurt.

"Sorry, Susan."

Bolan left the car wondering if he and this lady would ever cross paths again.

He knew they would.

Grimaldi commenced lift-off the moment Bolan was half inside the chopper's bubble front.

The pilot chuckled, gave his passenger a disparaging look.

"You sure do have a way with the ladies, boss. You sure do."

"I'd rather have that lady unconscious for a while than dead permanently."

"What a guy, throwing away a woman like that."

"I've got a feeling we haven't seen the last of her," Bolan growled, reaching for the radio transceiver on the chopper's dash control cluster.

"Where to?"

"The Farm, Jack, and don't spare the horses." Then, activating the transceiver, "Striker to Stony Man, come in Stony Man."

April's voice came over a backup shortwave setup at the Farm.

"This is Stony Man, go ahead Striker."

"I'm coming in. The hit will go down this morning before sunrise. Give it a ninety-nine percent probability. Commando unit, about twenty men."

"I'll pass the word."

"Anything turn up on that security scan on Captain Wade?"

"Negative. He appears to be clean all the way."

"Everyone is so clean but still there's so much dirt. Damn. Okay, lady, batten down the hatches. Jack and I are on our way in. Over and out."

"Hurry home, Striker. Over and out."

Static crackled in Bolan's headphones.

Grimaldi piloted the Hughes in a southwesterly course. The lights of residential Virginia thinned out as the flight took them over black patches of Blue Ridge mountain country. Toward Stony Man.

There was no inclination to talk.

A merc-gone-bad named Al Miller.

The next link in the chain.

Bolan would find Miller at Stony Man Farm.

He could have waited at the Farm all evening for Miller instead of tearing apart Wonderland on the Potomac, looking for the truth in a city of lies.

Sure.

Hindsight is 20-20.

But Bolan would have missed the privilege of dispatching the vermin he had encountered on this chase that was about to erupt at the very heart and soul of everything that meant anything to Bolan in his life as John Phoenix.

A commando assault on Stony Man Farm.

How many men had the Executioner killed this night?

Not nearly enough.

17

The undulating Blue Ridge terrain was magnified and rendered clear by the infrared binoculars, pitch-darkness turned into dusk hazed with a reddish glow.

Al Miller was splayed flat on a low knoll that interrupted the forest with a superb view of the killing ground.

From a point five hundred meters outside the Farm's perimeter, he slowly panned the acreage with the glasses, reconfirming the patterns of security established by Stony Man after the sabotage of their satellite-communications unit.

Personnel were working desperately down there to repair the unit.

Not that it will matter, thought the misguided merc.

"Not after tonight," he said aloud to himself.

Movement from his right. He dropped the binoculars to let them hang by their strap and whipped the Uzi around as he darted back to the base of a wide-trunked oak.

"Zebra alpha," he hissed into the darkness. Then he soundlessly switched positions in case someone wanted to fire at the sound of his voice.

"Ambrose tango," came a cautious whisper out of the early-morning gloom, and another commando approached Miller's position.

Pete Kagor and the rest of the team wore night-infiltration garb that matched Miller's. They were togged in black, faces camouflaged with black combat cosmetics, toting side arms, Uzis and grenades.

Kagor lay flat beside Miller.

"We're twenty seconds and counting."

"We'll give them five minutes to engage security," Miller said, continuing to view the Farm stretched out in the distance below their position.

"Five minutes? Jeffcoat expects us to follow through *two* minutes after he initiates."

"Jeffcoat is wrong."

"Hold it, Top. Those are good men."

Miller pulled his attention away from the binoculars to eyeball his second-in-command.

"You getting an attack of the conscience, suddenly? Kinda late for that, isn't it?"

"No one said we were going to sacrifice good men."

"It'll be worth it." Miller resumed his infrared pan of the terrain. "Those folks down below are going to respond fast. Faster than we think. Another three minutes will give their security that much additional time to pull extra forces into the fray at the airfield, and that's less warm bodies we'll have to kill on our way in."

"I understand your reasoning, but—"

"Aren't you getting paid enough, soldier?"

"Okay...okay, I'm getting paid enough," Kagor grunted. "But there are other ways—"

"Get to your goddamn post," Miller snarled. "We move in five minutes after Jeffcoat's team hits. Or do you want to argue about it?"

"I just don't think it's right."

"Fuck what you think is right," Miller hissed. "Git."

Kagor got.

Al Miller focused the infrared binoculars on the airfield situated two thousand meters inside the north perimeter of this secret base. He could see two hangars, camouflaged from air detection, and a runway. Two aircraft, a prop job and a chopper, sat on the airstrip. There would be more in the hangars.

Any second now.

Miller's attack force was deployed into six-man combat teams, as they had rehearsed for so long at the grounds of the Potomac estate. One team was waiting outside the Farm's north perimeter, not far from the airfield; another team was poised to strike from the southwest corner of the Farm.

The remaining team hid in the dense predawn darkness near Miller's present position.

Each team was equipped with two portable one-man grenade launchers. The teams had rehearsed to close in slowly, then group into two three-man squads with a pointman leading a squad by twenty paces.

These men were combat specialists, intensively trained by Miller for this one hit in all the arts of silent night killing. The grenade launchers would devastate any serious defense encountered by Miller's commando unit.

He intended tonight's action by this crew to be a standard hit-and-git night attack.

Jeffcoat's team would engage Stony Man forces at the air base.

Kagor's crew would hit from the southwest. Miller's own team would strike from this easterly position they now held. There would be casualties on Miller's side, he knew, but they would spread out around the Farm's command center, that innocent-appearing farmhouse in the middle of the acreage.

The Stony Man Phoenix project would be canceled forever.

And Al Miller would be a rich man.

They would all be rich men.

Those who survived.

Miller had learned his infiltration technique as a Green Beret in Vietnam. Covert actions in that war made it an easy step to work for the CIA when the war was over; the connections had already been made, and the Company knew Miller to be a ruthless specialist in the many arts of violent death.

Miller considered himself a success because he kept morals out of his professional work. His only morality was a big paycheck, and he had a healthy Swiss bank account full of hefty retainers as a specialist and adviser in such places as North Africa, El Salvador and Ireland.

On occasion he had played both sides against each

other, collecting two paychecks. That had taken a bit of fancy footwork. But it was nothing like tonight.

Miller glanced at the luminous hands of his wrist-watch.

One more minute.

Then . . . attack.

He focused the infrared binoculars one last time on the farmhouse.

Except for a few men working on the damaged satellite system, there was no movement. Lighted windows were well draped.

Miller knew most of the activity was underground. That subterranean section would be the most vital part of this hit . . . and the most difficult. But once their security force was dealt with, the house could be taken with the firepower his teams would rain down upon it.

He shifted the binoculars to make a final check uprange, where he could make out the nondescript guardhouse at the main entrance to the Farm, near the northeast corner of the sprawling property.

The guardhouse did not look fortified, although Miller knew it was. It didn't even look like a guardhouse, but it was manned by a team of crack troops, all heavily armed.

He could see nothing had changed since the last time he checked the guardhouse several minutes earlier. Security had been beefed up around the farmhouse and perimeter since the soft-probe sabotage, but Miller saw nothing that his team could not handle.

And Miller would be a rich man.

Tonight would pay off better than the last two overseas missions Miller had undertaken. And the fact that it was an internal squabble within his country's intel network did not mean a damn thing to Miller.

He had moved through this maze of spy shenanigans at home and abroad long and hard enough to know that this sort of thing happened now and then.

Besides, it was as good a way as any of weeding out those not strong enough to survive this kind of work.

Hell, if tonight's action meant a life of ease in some pleasure-spa with naked babes, good booze and gourmet food, why not?

Someone had to do it.

Sure, things would be hot for Al in and around D.C.—things would be hot for him everywhere—after tonight.

But enough bucks could buy a new face, a new identity, anything. . . and Miller was being paid more than enough for all that.

Miller thought about John Phoenix.

Was Phoenix here at Stony Man Farm at this moment? Not according to Miller's contact inside the Farm.

Miller knew all about Grover Jones—or whatever the hell Muslim name that jive dude called himself, thought Miller—and he knew Phoenix had evaded the ambush Jones had so sloppily arranged. If Phoenix hadn't killed that uppity bastard, I would've.

So where was Phoenix right now?

Miller brushed aside the concern.

The merc topkick replaced the glasses in the leather case strapped around his neck. He gripped the Uzi in preparation for action at the sounds of Jeffcoat's attack at the airstrip.

Sprawled on the knoll overlooking the dark Farm, ready for action, Al Miller experienced a sensual anticipation that was almost sexual.

He would kill people tonight. He would pull the trigger of the Uzi and listen to screams of fear and pleading dissolve as bullets shredded flesh and sprayed brains. Somehow the thought of death weirdly excited him for the woman at the house in Potomac. The bitch. Tied to a chair, waiting to take what he wanted before he quit that house and his country forever.

Where is Phoenix?

It didn't matter. Not one goddamn.

Phoenix was already too late to save Stony Man Farm.

WHERE IS MACK BOLAN?

It meant a lot to April Rose.

The mission controller of Stony Man Farm sat at the shortwave console of the command center, checking the load and action of her .44 Magnum for at least the tenth time since Bolan had kissed her at the airstrip before Grimaldi airlifted him off into the night.

April felt the same old concern gnawing her as it always did when her man was in the fire.

The fact that the fight was so close to home gave the concern a coolness that nibbled at the base of her spine.

She had relayed Mack's last message to the men of Phoenix Force, who were now in the com-room.

Yakov Katzenelenbogen and his team hustled out into the night to make last-minute checks and adjustments of the defense perimeter of the Farm.

Mack's initial assessment of the computer sabotage had been correct, as usual.

Stony Man Farm was about to be attacked.

That was something else that made a difference. So many times April sat and waited at this very console, giving Bolan intel support and coordinating the various Stony Man units. Most of the time April was out of action. But not tonight.

Not tonight.

She holstered the .44 and swiveled in her chair to face the array of hi-tech electronics just as Katz and David McCarter returned.

Both Phoenix Force members had procured M-16s to supplement their holstered side arms.

"Manning and Ohara are beefing up security around the airfield," Yakov told April. "Encizo is covering Kurtzman and his men."

"Any news from Bear?"

"A matter of minutes," McCarter reported.

Yakov set down his rifle and leaned against a nearby wall. He shook a cigarette out of a pack and lit it.

"That might be too long if Striker is correct about the hit coming down anytime. The hours right before dawn; the best time for a hit."

McCarter straddled a chair backward.

"Too bad the patrols we sent out didn't find anything."

"We couldn't afford to send them too far," Yakov reminded the Briton.

McCarter's face was taut with the anticipation of violence. "I hate like bloody hell having to sit here waiting for them to hit us. It should bleedin' well be the other way around."

"That's the way Mack has always felt," April agreed.

A strong attack is the best defense. Seek out the enemy and hit him first. Hit him when he isn't ready for you. Hit him hard. Hit him again and again. And be as merciless to him as he is to his victims.

Bolan and Jack Grimaldi, who should have landed at the Stony Man airstrip by now, were late.

They were late.

Where is Mack Bolan?

April Rose had no idea.

She had a funny thought. *I'd rather be right here than anywhere else in the world tonight, except for by his side.*

April had never felt the restless searching that supposedly guides everyone through their twenties, probably due to the same pragmatic nature that guided her to graduate summa cum laude from U of C at Berkeley with a bachelor's degree in electronics engineering and a master's in solid-state physics by the time she was twenty-two.

Her search had been for a satisfying role through

which to channel her knowledge and skills that she hoped, in however small a way, would contribute toward resolving some of the ills of humanity on this mixed-up planet.

She had not been interested in pursuing the high-fashion modeling career that had paid her way through college, though some of the offers seemed like the moon and the stars.

She had found her niche when she accepted an appointment with the U.S. Justice Department's Sensitive Operations Group that led directly to her association with Mack Bolan and her present position code-named Stony Man Two.

At twenty-nine years of age, April Rose was exactly where she wanted to be in her life.

Even tonight.

Especially tonight.

She found her first gray hair two days ago, and it hardly came as a surprise. But the more she put into the Stony Man operation, the more rewarding her life became.

Especially with a good man named Bolan who somehow seemed to give April everything she needed in every department of their relationship without ever crowding or wanting more than she could give.

April respected that more than anything else about her man, and she treated him the same way even though it hurt her more than she cared to admit each time her warrior left on another mission.

April had come a long way since childhood days as a sunshine kid in Modesto. Mom was gone two years now. April always managed to make it home to share Christmas and a week every summer with her father, a retired biology teacher. But beyond that her life revolved around the good souls and everything that mattered so much here at the nerve center of Mack's terrorist wars.

April Rose would go the distance for Mack Bolan.

Where is he? she wondered.

Perhaps he's wrong about the attack scheduled for tonight.

But she didn't think so.

The door to the communications room opened and Captain Wade strolled in. The security officer ignored Katz and McCarter. He stopped to face April at the console.

"Yes, Captain?"

"I've learned that my file has been subjected to a security scan at your request, Miss Rose."

She reacted coolly to the officer towering above her.

"That was routine."

"Routine, shit," growled Wade. "It was done under orders from Colonel Phoenix, wasn't it? That man didn't trust me worth a damn when he eyeballed me awhile ago. I resent that."

"Maybe you oughta take that up with the colonel, mate," McCarter suggested from across the room. "Give the lady a break, as you lads like to say."

"You might also try acting like a soldier," Katz put in. "Your place is with your men, Captain. This will go on your record."

The security officer glared at April.

"I want an answer."

April lifted a cautionary hand to the Phoenix Force men.

"I can handle this, gentlemen." She continued to address Wade. "Colonel Phoenix exercised his prerogative as your commanding officer to rescan your security clearance because of the vital nature of the position you hold. And this man is right, Captain. Your place is out there maintaining the security of this operation. Why are you behaving in this manner?"

Wade looked contrite.

"You're right, of course. Excuse me."

Before Wade could leave the room, a quadrant on an electronic security screen in front of April began to flash frantically, sequenced with an urgent buzzing alarm.

The perimeter of Stony Man Farm was wired for sound with amplifiers containing filters that screened out every sound except movement and voices. These were magnified more than two hundred times within the sixty-meter range of the devices.

"It's a hit," grunted Yakov Katzenelenbogen, starting for the door with his M-16.

"Come on," McCarter growled at Captain Wade as the Briton hustled along with Yakov. "It's time to scrap."

April Rose unleathered her .44 Magnum.

This time she was not to check anything; this time she would use it.

She could not take her eyes off the flashing quadrant on the screen.

They're hitting the airfield.

Stony Man Farm was under attack!

18

"Stony Man Farm is under attack," Hal Brognola informed the president of the United States. "That's what we got before all communication was cut off."

Brognola, the president and Lee Farnsworth had been joined by Brigadier General James Crawford, retired, for another top-secret Oval Office meeting to discuss the Phoenix situation, which now could only be regarded as critical.

The president scrutinized Farnsworth.

"What can you tell us about this, Lee?"

The CFB boss bristled but held himself in check, considering the source of the question.

"I assure you, sir, neither the Central Foreign Bureau nor I have anything to do with what is happening at Stony Man Farm tonight."

"Tell that to the men of Able Team in the goddamn Hindu Kush," Brognola grumbled.

"Stony Man has been unable to establish communications with those people?" asked the president.

"Afraid so, sir," Brognola reported. "Their contact point is a connection in New Delhi who monitors our signals. We've been unable to contact our man via satellite, of course, and we can't contact him any other way due to the, uh, highly sensitive nature of his cover. Able Team is still set to hit that fortress of The Dragon. Unless they already have, in which case they're all probably dead.''

''This is hardball, and they struck out,'' growled Farnsworth. He turned to the president, his tone softening respectfully. ''It just shows how in need we are of paring down our clandestine operations.''

The Man glanced at Hal.

''Is there any indication at all of the source of this attack on the Farm, who is responsible?''

''We don't know, sir. Colonel Phoenix is pursuing that area.''

''Where is Colonel Phoenix?''

''Uh, we don't know, sir,'' Brognola admitted.

''We're not the only ones who'd like to talk to Colonel Phoenix,'' said Farnsworth. ''The CIA is out for his hide.''

The president sighed.

''I guess I'd better hear the bloody details.''

''They are bloody, sir. The Company has an all points issued to its field personnel in the area regarding Phoenix. He walked into a setup the CIA had on some Armenian hit men who showed on the scene yesterday. Phoenix apparently figured the Armenians were tied in with this Stony Man thing, or he thought they might be involved and he wanted to confirm or deny. Several people were killed including one agent. His partner, an older man named Gridell, was wounded. The Company says it would not have happened if Phoenix had kept out of their operation.''

General Crawford had listened to all of this without missing a word or inflection. Now he joined the conversation.

"I've known Phoenix longer than any man in this room. I understand the man. I'm on his side one hundred percent. I, uh, actually have a personal interest in this, believe it or not."

The general briefly sketched for the others his encounter with Bolan when he brought Kelly Crawford home.

"I owe the man," the general continued. "But after what happened after he left my home, I must confess the best thing for security purposes would be for the colonel to come in immediately and cease all of this unsanctioned activity."

"Unsanctioned?" Brognola almost shouted. "Then I say we should damn well sanction it! I've known the man we call Phoenix quite awhile myself, and I know he's never killed anyone who didn't have it coming."

"I quite agree," nodded Crawford, "but that is immaterial in this case, Hal. I monitor the D.C. police. Of course they haven't put it together yet but the killer of three men in a black bar and at the scene of another homicide crosstown matches Colonel Phoenix to a *T*.

"I have the interests of Stony Man and the CFB in mind, believe me. I helped create both units. Which is why I believe Phoenix must come in. You know the way the media and the eager beavers on the Hill are these days.

"They practically destroyed the effectiveness of

our espionage apparatus during the seventies after Watergate to the point where it's barely been built back up to where it once was.

"And all of that is being jeopardized by Colonel Phoenix running all over D.C. wasting everyone he comes in contact with. If the local authorities stumble on to this, it's over. The press has the Department better wired than we do. No, I'm sorry, Hal. Phoenix must come in."

"And what about Stony Man Farm?" Hal asked the president.

The Man shook his head.

"I'm sorry, Hal. You're asking the impossible. I can't order troops in to protect an installation that doesn't exist. Neither can anyone else. That has always been the case."

Brognola was angry enough to yank out a cigar and light it. Fuck the president if he didn't like smokers and there were no ashtrays. The ashes would have to be dropped on the goddamn floor and if they wanted him to leave, he would be damn glad for the fresh air.

Stony Man Farm.

Under attack.

Mack Bolan.

Out there in the night, and if the Executioner did not obey an order from the Man there would damn well be a liquidation order issued on Phoenix by his own government.

The men of Able Team.

Lyons, Schwarz and Blancanales had already bought it, or soon would, because Stony Man could not warn them of a trap set by The Dragon.

And Hal Brognola.

Who could not help.

He had to get to Stony Man Farm as quickly as possible. He used a White House phone to call April Rose.

"April, it's Hal. I'm coming in." That was all he said before he hung up.

ABLE TEAM HAD TRUDGED their way across the unforgiving Himalayan rocks for five hard days, following the directions of a source they were not sure they could trust in the Pakistani frontier settlement of Peshawar.

Now Able Team was ready to hit.

The Dragon's lair continued the straight rise of a deep gorge that widened into a craggy valley on either side of the Stony warriors. The men crouched against slablike rock at the base of the gorge several hundred feet below the castle.

It was midmorning but an earlier reconnaissance gave the three men reason to believe that this place, the wall above the gorge, was the enemy's weakest point since they expected no attack up the face of the gorge.

The enemy did not know that Carl Lyons had been an avid climber in the Sierra Nevadas. Rosario "Politician" Blancanales and Hermann "Gadgets" Schwarz, the Bolan sidekicks from Nam, had undergone intensive mountain-climbing training during the early days of the Stony Man program.

And all three men were in excellent physical condition.

Able Team's scouting trip of The Dragon's castle and terrain also convinced them of the urgency to strike *now*, daylight or no.

There had been no sign of activity in or around the castle.

It was as if The Dragon, whoever the hell he was, had been alerted or had for some other reason pulled his forces out of the area.

The ancient castle had originally been owned by some long-forgotten warlord. His legacy had found use today at the hands of someone called The Dragon, who trafficked in mass death and destruction for blood money.

The Dragon had to be taken out. The action was authorized by Stony Man.

Able Team must penetrate the castle, but they had to confirm that the enemy had fled. If they had pulled out, Able Team would scramble damn fast to pick up any trail The Dragon might have left.

Each team member was armed with a shoulder-holstered MAC-10 submachine gun and had an M-16 strapped across his back. They were each equipped with climbing picks, ropes and accessories that they unpacked.

"Wonder why you couldn't reach the contact in New Delhi on that radio," Lyons whispered with a nod to the shortwave set Schwarz was carrying.

"Something is going down," said Gadgets. "Our contact has the jitters."

"He'd answer if Stony Man had any messages for us," said Blancanales.

"What an optimist," grunted Lyons. "All right, men. Let's do it and do it right."

Mack Bolan's Able Team broke off all conversation.

They commenced climbing the face of the gorge.

Not knowing what they would find.

19

Grimaldi brought the Hughes chopper through the low cloud cover. The clouds would mute sounds of the helicopter's approach.

Bolan and Grimaldi had donned infrared Nitefinder eye shields.

In a night action, the Executioner always tried to think like the enemy.

What was the only conceivably vulnerable point on the Farm, near the perimeter?

"Come in low over the airfield from the north," Bolan instructed the pilot.

Grimaldi tugged the stick to bring the copter in at a low banking approach.

The night suddenly boomed.

The sky lit up briefly as a blast erupted below.

As Grimaldi sailed in, Bolan heard the crackle of automatic-weapons fire and claps from two more HEs.

The chopper emerged from the clouds. Grimaldi piloted them in low enough for the Nitefinders to reveal that the assault had just begun.

The airfield shimmered in an eerie golden glow from the flaming pile of junk that had moments earlier been a helicopter on the runway.

The firelight inadvertently cast flickering illumination on two squads of commandos Bolan could see advancing on the hangars in a wedgelike formation. Two of the commandos were in the process of reloading portable grenade launchers. The six infiltrators charged across the clearing separating the tree line from the hangars.

The illumination was enough for a dozen security troops, waiting behind the hangars, to more clearly see the infiltrators and open up with M-16s.

Bolan made out two members of Phoenix Force, Keio Ohara and Gary Manning, flanking off to either side of the Farm security forces, opening fire with their automatic weapons to catch the commando infiltrators from two new angles of fire.

The commando squads hastily fanned away from each other as the barrage cut down the two pointmen.

One of the invaders triggered his grenade launcher.

The side of one hangar disintegrated into a sheet of flame as bodies of soldiers rained to the ground.

Ohara and Manning directed fierce streams of automatic fire at the source of the HE. Another commando spun every which way at once as his head and guts exploded.

The three surviving infiltrators fell back to regroup.

The Hughes chopper zipped overhead with Bolan bracing himself in the open door of the bubble front.

The Executioner unleashed a rain of death from the M-16 Grimaldi always kept in the chopper.

Two of the darting commandos kept on moving,

even after the stream of 5.56mm fire decapitated them, sending chunks of their skulls and brains splashing into the air ahead of them.

The third commando had time to turn and look up at the Hughes zooming by, twenty feet above his head. He had time to start tracking the Uzi upward.

But he had time to do nothing else. The downdraft from the rotors made standing unsteady.

Bolan fired another burst from the M-16, and the guy was poleaxed backward off his feet with a shocked expression and no chest.

The troops around the hangars held their fire as the Hughes climbed and pulled away.

"Swing us around the southwest perimeter and back along the eastern side," Bolan instructed the ace pilot.

Grimaldi did that. It took all of thirty seconds for the sweep, for Bolan to analyze Al Miller's strategy.

The infiltrators on the ground simply froze in place amid the shadowy shapes of trees, shrubs and changes in the terrain as the Hughes skimmed by overhead. They had no way of knowing the chopper's occupants were using infrared equipment and could clearly spot every one of them.

The strategy was clear. Miller was operating with three teams on this assault. One team hit the airfield. The other two waited until the airfield alert drew additional security troops. Then Miller's other teams would move in.

Bolan saw sporadic exchanges of fire between commandos and security patrols who attempted to intercept them. But it was too damn dark down there. Bolan saw one terrorist go down. He saw two Farm troopers spin away to the ground under hails of enemy fire.

When the chopper had made a complete circle, Bolan got Stony on the shortwave.

"Striker to Stony Man."

April's voice. "Stony Man. Go ahead, Striker."

"I'm coming in from the outside," said Bolan. "Five infiltrators moving in on the main building from the southwest. They're meeting some resistance. Get them reinforced."

"I'll send Katz and McCarter. Anything else?"

"Eight more moving in from the east. Have Wade send down anyone he can spare from the front gate. I'm moving in on the eight. Over and out."

Bolan felt good hearing April's voice. What a woman.

Grimaldi did not need telling. He swung the chopper in low behind the eight figures advancing from the east.

The commandos were a thousand meters from the main house when they were engaged in a firefight with security troops.

The predawn night of Stony Man Farm crackled with sounds of armed combat, men grunting terse exchanges, the cacophony of battle echoing back from the low cloud ceiling heavy with a rain that would not come.

Shadows darted between shadows.

Flashes of gunfire lanced the thick black air.

As Grimaldi zoomed in, Bolan saw one of the com-

mandos nailed to a tree by a blast of M-16 automatic
fire from one of the Stony Man security men.

There was no sign of Wade.

Bolan was back in the doorway of the chopper
when the Hughes raced over two wedge-shape squads
of commandos and two other men lagging somewhat
behind.

The straggling pair would be Miller and his second-
in-command.

Miller was the next link in the chain. He had to be
taken alive.

Bolan opened fire with his M-16 at the two forward squads. He saw four of the men caught in a
withering hail of fire. The other two, and Miller and
his man, scattered. Bolan lost sight of Miller behind a
clump of trees as the chopper started to climb away.

One of the surviving commandos swung around
his grenade launcher, aimed at the receding chopper
and triggered.

The chopper rocked and spun as the night erupted
for Bolan in a thunderclap of brilliance and spinning
sensation.

The chopper was hit!

Grimaldi had been cruising low enough so that
Bolan's fall to the meadow would jolt every bone in
his body, but not enough to kill him.

Bolan came out of a tumbling roll in time to see the
chopper skid to a stop in the clearing several feet
away. Grimaldi was able to land the damaged aircraft, but he did not emerge from the disabled
Hughes.

Bolan had lost the M-16 somewhere during his fall.

Though he still wore the Nitefinder goggles he did not take time to look for the rifle.

He unleathered his .44 AutoMag and raced toward the chopper while keeping a constant lookout for any movement coming at him. There was none. The Hughes had sustained a hit to its rear end, which was now in flames.

The fuel tank could go at any moment.

Bolan reached the bubble front and found Grimaldi slumped forward against his shoulder-strap harness. The pilot wore a nasty bruise on his temple.

Bolan unhooked the man who had saved the Executioner's hide on so many missions. Jack was breathing.

Bolan kept Big Thunder in his right fist, fanning the night as he hefted the Stony flyboy over his shoulder and jogged away from the fiery wreck.

He went twenty paces when the Nitefinders caught a figure to his left. It was the bastard who'd brought down the chopper. The guy was swinging an Uzi around in Bolan's direction, not particularly careful to stand behind cover because he didn't know Bolan could see him.

Bolan did not slacken his pace as he brought up Big Thunder and triggered a .44 Magnum round that ruptured the guy's head into a reddish mist in the infrared goggles.

Behind them, the Hughes exploded as the fire touched the fuel. A hot invisible wall lifted Bolan and his human cargo off the ground then slammed them back down.

APRIL ROSE EMERGED from the "farmhouse" command post in time to catch Katz and McCarter. She relayed to them Bolan's report of the number and position of infiltrators moving in from the southwestern corner of the Farm.

"Wade's chaps need backup," McCarter grunted, snicking his M-16 into its automatic mode.

"Let's give it to them," growled Katzenelenbogen.

The two Phoenix members hustled off into the night.

April gripped her pistol. She had no intention of returning to the safety of the Stony Man communications room. The farmhouse was adequately guarded.

She turned and jogged back to the grounds on the other side of the house where Phoenix Force member Rafael Encizo was covering Aaron Kurtzman and his men in their final repairs of the sabotaged satellite unit.

The rattle of gunfire and an exploding HE broke the darkness.

She advanced on the tight circle of men and equipment several meters behind the farm building.

April sensed movement to her right.

Crouching, she whirled and fired the Magnum in a two-handed grip. She clearly saw the figure of a commando and heard the sound of a bullet slapping open flesh and bone, and a grunt of expelled breath and the rustle of deadweight tripping backward to the ground.

They were getting close. This one must have circled around from the eastern squads engaged by Bolan and Grimaldi!

April Rose continued cautiously toward Kurtzman, Encizo and the others to see what she could do.

McCarter and Katzenelenbogen came upon heavy fire when they were about one thousand meters from the house.

They found three of Captain Wade's security personnel pinned down and exchanging fire with the enemy across a clearing of dogwood. One security man was sprawled in a lifeless clump where he fell, a dark pool of blood around his head.

"Colonel Phoenix got one of them, sir," a lieutenant reported to Katz. "I think two of them split off to circle around us or the house. That leaves three across that meadow, and we're too damn pinned down to budge or do anything but hold them up."

Katz plucked a grenade from his utility belt.

"The pot needs stirring," he told the soldier who was not outfitted with grenades.

"Give it to 'em, mate," growled McCarter.

The Briton had pitched himself onto his belly alongside the soldiers and was returning fire at the two blasting commandos across the clearing.

Katz pulled out the pin with his teeth. He flung the explosive with his prosthetic right hand. The grenade sailed true. The Phoenix team members and soldiers ducked, covering their eyes.

Ten seconds after the pin was pulled, the HE ruptured the night in a dazzling flash of fire, smoke and roar that flung the shredded remains of two commandos high into the air like the remnants of rag dolls chewed up and discarded by a playful pup.

One commando emerged from behind a rise in the

terrain and opened fire with his Uzi. Two of the Stony Man soldiers grunted and were flung back, the tops of their heads blown away.

McCarter, Katz and the lieutenant opened fire simultaneously.

The commando burst apart under the sheet of automatic M-16 fire as if drawn and quartered.

BOLAN SET DOWN Grimaldi's unconscious form at the base of a towering oak. Jack was still out of it, but he was wearing a .45 holstered cross-draw at his left hip. He would be okay once he came to. Until then, this appeared to be a safe spot for the stricken pilot.

As Grimaldi had been setting down the Hughes, the rattle of gunfire in the night seemed to Bolan to have closed in toward the main house of the installation.

Guided by his infrared eye shield, Bolan started off through the night in the direction of the farmhouse, across another rolling and dipping ten acres.

He had to find Miller.

Alive.

Who had ordered this attack?

Bolan intended to find out from the commando merc boss.

One way or another.

The Executioner traveled soundlessly for about twenty meters when his peripheral infrared vision caught sight of an Uzi-toting commando who thought he had enough cover behind a tree.

Bolan fired. The .44 headbuster tore through skullbone and brains and snuffed another existence. The dead commando was kicked back from behind his tree by the impact of the slug. He slammed into another tree behind him. Then he pitched forward to the earth and did not move.

The Executioner moved on.

AL MILLER COULD TELL his men were being blasted apart by the way the gunfire in the distance, punctuated by a grenade blast now and then, died off to nothing. The farmhouse and the crew around the outbuilding where the satellite repairs were taking place had not yet been attacked. That meant trouble.

The commando leader and Kagor crouched on a knoll northwest of the farmhouse and the cluster of people.

Miller observed the repair crew—a big bear of a man, a Latin American and some soldiers standing guard—and debated the best way for him and Kagor to hit them. Then they could pull out to the west and would have a good shot at getting away even if the hit teams were in tatters.

After the helicopter had been downed—at least Miller now had a good idea where John Phoenix was!—Miller and Kagor had circled around to the north, cutting over short of the Stony Man airstrip and carefully moving west until they reached the knoll.

Miller cursed his bad luck. But he had been in hotspots such as this one and walked away.

Well, maybe not *this* hot, he thought. Not if Phoenix was still prowling around out there in the night.

Had Phoenix been killed when the chopper crashed?

Miller had a hunch the big man was damn near indestructible!

Kagor, crouched next to Miller, motioned with the snout of his Uzi at the men around the outbuilding.

"What the hell are we waiting for?" he demanded in a whisper. "Looks like we're alone on this one, Top."

"We could still have some backup. Some of the boys could've slipped through. Okay, let's hit this bunch. Be careful, K. Careful for that goddamn Phoenix."

"Phoenix?" snickered Kagor. "He was kil—"

Kagor was interrupted by a stutter of Uzi fire across the clearing from where Miller and he lay watching.

Miller swung his infrared binoculars to see one of his own commandos rattling off the steady stream of hot lead at the circle of people around the sabotaged satellite unit. Miller saw one Stony Man trooper fly back until he fell, as if tripped. The others scattered, except for one Hispanic down there with an M-16.

Miller placed the man from the intel his contact inside the Farm had furnished: Rafael Encizo, member of Bolan's Phoenix Force.

The commando started to dodge back for cover when Encizo swung around his M-16.

The commando made it halfway to the shelter of some trees when Encizo loosed a burst that pulped out the commando's back and turned his run into a stagger that became a fall into hell.

The bearlike man—Kurtzman, thought Miller—emerged from cover and returned to his work.

"Take them *now*," Miller hissed.

The attention of Encizo and the others was drawn to the direction from which the commando had just opened fire. The group's unprotected flank was toward the knoll that hid Miller and Kagor.

The mission can still be saved, thought Miller. This bunch are sitting ducks. They're already dead, only they don't know it. Two or three grenades into the farmhouse, and we pull out.

Without leaving their cover the two remaining merc commandos sighted their Uzis on Encizo, Kurtzman and the other Stony Man people.

Miller and Kagor opened fire.

And more death blistered the night.

20

When the twin volley of Uzi rapidfire sprayed its death hail at Kurtzman and the others, Mack Bolan was halfway from the tree line of the clearing around the house to where the repairs were being done near the outbuilding. The ambushers were hidden from Bolan's infrared line of vision.

The pair were not aware of Bolan's approach.

This would be Al Miller and his second-in-command! Bolan was sure of it.

Bolan the nightscorcher jogged around to their flank.

He saw several things at once.

He saw a Stony Man security soldier and Aaron Kurtzman crumple to the ground as Uzi gunfire ripped them apart.

The soldier fell and did not move.

Kurtzman looked badly hit. He was thrashing around. Some of his crew rushed to help him.

Rafael Encizo had lightning reflexes. The Phoenix Forcer swung around his M-16 and fired at the knoll where the ambush had come from. The slugs from the M-16's automatic fire ricocheted off dirt and trees, but the firing from the Uzis had already stopped.

Bolan saw two commandos dart from their cover and dash west an instant before Encizo opened fire at where they had been.

Bolan started to head off Miller and his companion. He would blow off an arm or a leg if he had to, but he would stop those two and take them alive, and they would talk. Bolan hoped like hell that Kurtzman hadn't checked out for good.

Before he could close in on the retreating commandos, Bolan also sighted Captain Wade. The Stony Man security officer caught sight of Miller and the other commando in the distant lights from the farmhouse.

Wade stood in their way and brought up the M-16.

"Captain Wade, hold your fire!" snapped Bolan.

Too late.

The commando leading the way—it would have to be Miller, thought Bolan—heard the shout, saw Wade and died.

Wade gave Al Miller a figure eight of gutshredding lead that lifted him off the ground, spun him around while he was airborne and slammed him facedown into his own blood.

The other commando loosed a short burst from his Uzi.

The spray of tumblers made dull little pops as they stitched a ragged line of holes across Captain Wade's chest. Half a dozen rounds kicked the security officer backward. He maintained a grip on his chattering M-16 for two or three seconds before he toppled back into some shrubbery and out of sight.

That last burst of slugs stitched the last commando

from crotch to neck, killing him on his feet. The man's knees buckled, and he crumpled to the ground.

Another boom rumbled across the Blue Ridge landscape to accompany the first grayish rays of dawn on the eastern horizon.

This time it really was thunder.

A fine mist began.

Bolan did not holster the stainless-steel AutoMag. He did pause long enough to pump a fresh magazine into the butt.

Rafael Encizo approached him from where Kurtzman and the others had been ambushed.

Guess I was wrong about Wade.

Then someone emerged from the farmhouse and also approached Bolan. His heart skipped one beat as it always did whenever he saw April Rose.

She and Rafael reached Bolan at the same time.

Bolan gave Encizo a relieved brother-grip handshake.

He gave April one healthy hug and a kiss on those lovely full lips.

"Welcome home, soldier," she whispered shyly, and her eyes, close to his, said it came from the bottom of her soul.

Bolan kept an arm around April's waist. He didn't feel like ever letting go, but his eyes were iced when he glanced at Encizo.

"How's Bear?"

"Not good," grunted Encizo. "Looks like he caught two. One in the gut, one along the temple but we can't tell how deep. Doctor from the house is with him now . . . but it doesn't look good."

The rains came. The sky rumbled again and a breeze came up when the mist turned to showers. The slanting rain drifted across the new day's first light to the east and pattered across these combatants and felt real good.

Bolan looked at the beauty hugged against him.

"Able Team?" he asked.

"Bear got our satellite linkage restored just when the attack started," April told him. "They were putting finishing touches on the repairs when...the ambush got them. Bear had already sent me back inside to contact our man in New Delhi. Able Team hit The Dragon's fortress before we could reach them."

Rafael Encizo chuckled when he saw the grim look come into Phoenix's face.

"It's not what you think, Colonel. I guess we forgot who we were dealing with. The Dragon got away and left some firepower behind to eliminate Able Team. Trouble is, he didn't leave enough. Able took what The Dragon left for them and spit out the pieces."

April Rose saw something over Bolan's shoulder. Her eyes widened frantically, and she held out a hand.

"Don't—"

The woman moved suddenly in Mack Bolan's arm, swinging around to his left side at the same instant a sharp, single gun report punctuated the sounds of the rain.

April emitted a piercing scream and became a deadweight back in Bolan's left arm. He wrapped his left arm tighter around her to keep her from falling, knowing already what had happened.

Oh, God, no, he thought. *No!*

Balancing the weight of the woman with his left arm, the Executioner whirled in a bent-knee crouch.

The security officer, Wade, was flattened out on the ground where he fell after being shot, except that Wade wore a bullet-proof vest. He had killed Miller and the other commando to prevent them from talking and exposing him. He wasted them then got sloppy thinking he could put a bullet in Colonel John Phoenix.

April had seen Wade "rise from the dead" and aim the .45 at Mack. She had stepped in the way of the bullet.

Although Wade was not hurt, the impact must have rattled him. Now he leaned against an oak, shifting the Army issue .45 for another fast shot at Bolan.

The Executioner triggered the faithful .44 five times. His marksmanship was so accurate, the last four shots encountered nothing except bark.

The first slug had blown away Wade's head.

The lifeless body slid to the base of the tree, the ancient oak too stately to be his gravestone, the hieroglyphics, made by the bullet holes a fitting epitaph.

Then Bolan looked back at the woman he held.

April's head was resting on his shoulder, the way she always did when they relaxed during those infrequent moments of intimacy between his missions.

Never again....

He could not see the wound. He was glad for that. Her eyes were closed as though she were asleep. The rain washed her hair of blood.

The rain washed away his tears as Mack Bolan looked skyward at those stormy heavens. He was not aware of the activity around him.

Part of his world had ended.

"They'll pay," he vowed to a dead woman and to a universe that rumbled its foreboding thunder in response. "Whoever is responsible for this...I'll track them to the ends of the earth. They will pay."

DON PENDLETON ON
MACK BOLAN

From the front cover to the inside story, *Day of Mourning* is decidedly different. It is the first book in a trilogy that includes the next Super Bolan, *Terminal Velocity*, and #64, *Dead Man Running*. You can identify the books in the trilogy by their covers, which have red foil on the Mack Bolan name. Also available will be #63, *The New War Book*, an illustrated manual that brings readers right up to date on the history of Mack.

The trilogy begins a terrifying but triumphant new life for Bolan. He is about to become a fugitive in every nation on earth. But the enemy is the same: Savage Man, the slime-bucket of our violent streets who, by direct action or by manipulation, loots and pillages and rapes and extorts. We all know that the KGB is the biggest and most ruthless subversion machine the world has ever seen, and many of us also know that since 1961 there have been continual suspicions among senior counterintelligence operatives that the KGB has placed agents in the loftiest positions of U.S. power. Now Mack Bolan, peacemonger without peer, enters this darkest hell to prove that one man *can* make a difference. But he'll need help, and he'll get it—this will surprise you—from Aaron "The Bear" Kurtzman....

Meanwhile Mack's men of Able Team and Phoenix Force continue to operate out of Stony Man Farm under Hal Brognola's leadership. I have a feeling that The Executioner's fans are identifying one hundred percent with these teams' commitment to selfless ideals. By cheering the guys on, the reader's own sense of personal dignity and respect for life is deeply enhanced.

Don Pendleton

Our readers write about Mack Bolan

"The first Mack Bolan book I ever saw I read in one day—now I'm a collector. They are the best books I've ever read!"

—*C.L.,*Pittsburg, CA*

"Reading The Executioner really brings the newspaper headlines to life."

—*M.C., Poughkeepsie, NY*

"I stick with things I like. As long as you keep writing, I'll keep reading your books!"

—*S.F., NAS Pensacola, FL*

"Like a skillful surgeon, Mack Bolan cuts out the cancer of our society so the healthy community can grow. More than once, Mack has helped me to step back and re-examine my perspectives on life."

—*K.F., Cedar Springs, MI*

"Mack Bolan is a *human* hero, with deep feelings and a real soul."

—*A.B., Zion, IL*

"Thank you for hours of reading enjoyment and for the many more still to come."

—*T.D., Spokane, WA*

*Names available on request

GOLD
EAGLE